FAUJI BANTA SINGH

FAUJI

BANTA

SINGH

and other stories

by

Sadhu Binning

We acknowledge the support of the Canada Council for the Arts for our publishing program. We also acknowledge support from the Government of Ontario through the Ontario Arts Council.

We acknowledge the financial support of the Government of Canada through the Canada Book Fund for our publishing activities.

  ONTARIO ARTS COUNCIL
CONSEIL DES ARTS DE L'ONTARIO   Canada

Cover design by Peggy Stockdale

Binning, Sadhu
[Short stories. Selections]
    Fauji Banta Singh and other stories / Sadhu Binning.

ISBN 978-1-927494-25-7 (pbk.)

    I. Title.

PS8603.I62A6 2013   C813'.6   C2013-904887-1

Printed and bound in Canada by Coach House Printing

TSAR Publications
P. O. Box 6996, Station A
Toronto, Ontario M5W 1X7
Canada

www.tsarbooks.com

For
Pavel and Janik

Contents

Safe-keeping

SECONDS AFTER THE SCHOOL BELL RANG, a flood of kids quickly moved through the wide halls towards the three main doors leading out. One group of senior students was passionately debating the nuclear arms race, an issue they had discussed in class. Some kids were making faces at a girl coming down the hall, for no apparent reason. The mood was noisy and boisterous, there was a sense of joy about. However, Sito, a grade-twelve student, walked alone, uninterested in the life around her. She had come to school after several days of pretending to be sick and was glad that her friend Lucy had not been in school today. Lucy would ask too many questions to which she had no answers.

She reached the edge of the school grounds, all alone. On Fraser Street, the large window displays of colourful dresses outside the clothing stores failed to excite her. She fixed her eyes on the ground and paid no attention to the people around her or the cars that sped by. She stopped at the traffic light just as automatically as the light itself functioned. Her home was a little over a mile from school. It had always seemed to take only a few minutes to walk home; today it was taking forever.

The familiar melody of a car horn made her jump then filled her with hateful rage. She looked at the red Mustang wishing she could blow it into pieces. She wanted to shout out to the world the deception and humiliation she had suffered from the owner of that car. She wished for some miracle to erase all that had happened in the last few months. Trembling with hatred, she turned her face away and started to walk faster.

It was a bright and warm Monday afternoon. The sun shone over the beautiful city and Sito could see the snow-covered peaks glowing on the mountains in North Vancouver. There was a springlike freshness in the air. But it was not just the sun that made her cheerful; she was hoping to see the boy she had seen in the gurdwara yesterday. She had caught him secretly looking at her several times, during the religious readings of the Holy Granth. Later, while they stood in separate lines for food, she felt an electric current pass through her body when her eyes met his. He was the most handsome boy she had ever seen. The way he smiled, with his lips and eyes, captivated her.

Sito found his name from a cousin who lived in Kamloops and knew his sister: Kelly, short for Kulwant. She repeated it in her mind many times and tasted the sweet music in that name, Kelly.

She could hardly wait for school to end. She knew that many Punjabi boys drove around in their cars looking at girls walking on Fraser Street at the end of the school day. Her eyes searched for Kelly as she walked with her classmates, all busy talking, laughing, and watching the window displays in the clothing stores. When she saw him drive by in his red Mustang, her smile became a full-fledged laugh. He drove by again, screeching his tires, leaving behind a cloud of smoke and dust. She felt important, knowing that he was trying to impress her.

Sito intentionally walked slower and fell behind her classmates. Her best friend Lucy stayed with her; she was the only person Sito could confide in. They were in the same grade, shared a number of classes, and lived on the same street, two blocks away from each other. They had instantly become friends when Lucy moved to Vancouver from Williams Lake a year ago. Coming from a Punjabi background, Sito had always felt like an alien with most of the white girls in elementary and high school. But she didn't feel that way with Lucy. Sito had excitedly told Lucy about seeing Kelly in the gurdwara. Lucy was surprised to hear Sito talk about a boy. She had always been critical of girls who had boyfriends.

Every day after school, Sito had to rush home to prepare meals for her father and brother, who came back from work at four-thirty. They worked in the Silvertree sawmill, half a mile away from their home. Her mother worked the evening shift in St Mary's Hospital and had to change two buses to get to work. She usually left before Sito came home from school. Sito disliked this time of the day. She could not sit down to watch TV or do her homework, as her friends did. She couldn't even have the radio on, because her father and brother didn't like it. Today, however, she ran around with new energy and excitement. Seeing Kelly drive by over and over had given her immense but secret pleasure.

She was startled by the loud ring of the phone on the kitchen wall as she was cutting the onions to prepare the dal. Her heart pounded. She knew it was not Lucy, who always called her at exactly ten after four.

There was no answer to her hello. She said hello again and

this time a low voice asked, "Is this Sito?" She knew it was Kelly. He said, "Sito, I love you," and quickly hung up. This was the first time in her life that a boy had called her. She was terrified and yet filled with pleasure. She forgot about the onions she was cutting and began to fantasize. She saw herself as a heroine of a Hindi film, walking along with the singing hero in a beautiful garden. She closed her eyes and imagined herself in Kelly's strong arms.

But she was simply too scared to continue her fantasy, even though no one else was home at the time. Suddenly she became horrified: suppose somebody else had picked up the phone? What if her mom and dad found out about this? She was especially afraid of her brother, who always talked about how young Punjabi girls were being corrupted by the influence of western society.

Then there was the letter that her dad had received from a relative in India, who wanted Sito to sponsor his son to Canada as her husband. Sito's bedroom was next to the kitchen where her mom and dad always sat talking late at night. Recently she heard her dad saying, "The boy's family have a lot of land and they are well respected in the village. The boy has gone to college for two years. We cannot afford to lose such a nice match for Sito. Now is the right time to act." Her mother agreed.

Kelly phoned her again the same time the next day but hung up before she could say anything. That didn't surprise her because she knew he was afraid. She also understood the danger in her calling. If her father and brother came to know that Kelly was phoning her or following her on her way home from school, they would harm him and immediately take her out of school. Still, she couldn't help thinking about him—his handsome face, dark black hair, and large eyes.

A few days later on a Sunday morning she was watching TV

in her living room. Her mom and dad had gone to the gurd-wara and her brother was still sleeping. She saw Kelly walking on the street in front of her home. She was dumbfounded. "My heart was beating so fast, I thought, Oh God, if it beat any faster it would fly out of my body," she told Lucy the following day.

Lucy asked the same question she had asked many times before, "But why would your parents object? What would they do if you were to go home and tell them about Kelly today?"

"They'd kill me."

"But why?"

"It's simply not done." Sito wanted to, but didn't tell Lucy about her parents' plan to bring someone from India to marry her.

"If you ask me, I think you're lucky to have a handsome guy like Kelly interested in you. And I think your parents should be happy too."

"That'll be the day." They walked in silence for a while. "Lucy, what do you think I should do?"

"I think you should do what you want. You're not a kid any-more. For Christ's sake, in a few months we'll be graduating and looking for jobs."

"But how can I make my parents understand?"

"You aren't doing anything wrong. They will have to see that. Besides, remember what we were told in the socials. When you're eighteen you can do whatever you want with your life. Parents can't control you forever."

Lucy gave Sito advice that she felt was only common sense. Sito knew all this too, but to go against her family was unthink-able.

As the weeks passed and the daffodils came into bloom, Sito saw Kelly almost every day, either driving his red Mustang or walking by her on Fraser Street. At home and at school, she dreamt about him. Her dreams were always about the marriage ceremony. She saw herself in a red wedding suit walking behind Kelly around the Guru Granth Sahib.

She believed that when two people fall in love it must lead to marriage. And she never doubted that Kelly would have any problem accepting her as his bride. She didn't like Lucy's suggestion when she said, "Sito, to be honest with you, I don't like the way he behaves. If he's really interested in you, then why does he sneak around and call you on the phone and hang up like a jerk?"

Tears welled up in Sito's eyes and she avoided looking directly at Lucy. "You are just like the rest of them. You don't understand, things are different in our Punjabi culture. A guy just can't walk up to a girl and say whatever is on his mind."

"I am sorry if I hurt your feelings, but I just don't understand the game. What is he waiting for?"

"I guess he is waiting for some kind of signal from me."

Sito's parents wanted to marry her off as soon as she finished school, which was only a few months away. She felt sick to her stomach that she would be married to a person she had never seen before. If she could tell her parents that she knew someone, a boy who was also from a Punjabi family, they might listen to her. Her father might even know Kelly's family.

She decided to meet Kelly but she couldn't find enough courage to talk to him herself. She asked Lucy if she could talk to him.

Lucy stopped Kelly on the road one day and arranged their first meeting. Sito went to a park nearby during lunch break at school. Kelly was waiting for her and opened the passenger door from inside. She felt as if she were committing a crime, and before getting into the car she looked around to make sure no one was watching her.

They drove to a quiet street that passed through a cemetery. Lined with rows of tall trees on both sides, it seemed like a place far removed from the city. They sat quietly looking out over the field of tombstones.

"Why do you follow me around?" Sito asked timidly, not knowing exactly what to say.

"I think you are the most beautiful thing that God ever made and I love you," Kelly replied. His low voice was like sweet music to her ears. Sito hesitated for a second then let him hold her hand as he slowly lifted it from her lap.

"How come I had never seen you before?" asked Sito.

"Oh, I was working in a small town near Kamloops and just moved here a couple of weeks before you saw me at the gurdwara the other day."

"How did you get my phone number so quickly?"

"I have my sources."

"It is my cousin from Kamloops who gave you my number, isn't it? I thought so. She is such a goof."

"Never mind about her," Kelly said. He held her at the shoulders and tried to draw her towards him to kiss her. She politely pushed him away.

Sito looked at her watch. "Oh God, look at the time. I have to go or I'll get into trouble."

"Okay, I won't try to kiss you but please stay for a while and talk to me." They sat quietly for a few moments.

"You have a nice car, so what do you do?" asked Sito.

"I finished high school two years ago. Yes, the class of nineteen seventy-one. Now I work the night shift in a factory, and I am also taking a welding course at the Vancouver Vocational Institute. What else do you want to know?"

Sito said, laughing, "A lot more yet."

She told Lucy everything as they walked home after school that day. They both agreed that Kelly was perfect for her.

Sito heard her parents discuss her marriage again that night. Her mother said, "Before we make plans for her marriage, we should ask her if she wants to go to college or learn some kind of trade."

Her father replied, "No, I think that we should marry her off immediately. If she wants to study more, she can do it later. You know that boy's family won't wait much longer and I suspect there are a couple of other families here who are interested in him. After all, they're the biggest land holders in their village and he is the only son, so he is going to inherit all that land."

Lying in her bed in her room, Sito thought about Kelly and wished she had the courage to tell her father about him. But if she were to take a bold step like that, would Kelly back her up? She needed to make sure.

Sito met Kelly again. He tried to take her to a friend's apartment but she refused. She remembered Lucy's warning, "Don't ever go to a place where he can take advantage of you, unless you yourself are ready for it." He took her to a restaurant on the other side of town. She was scared the whole time that she might be spotted.

The next time they met, she agreed to go to the apartment with Kelly, hoping to talk to him about marriage in a quieter and more private place. Once inside the apartment, he grabbed her and tried to force a kiss on her lips, moving his hands all over her body. Sito broke away from his grip and said, "First we have to talk."

"We'll talk later; let me hold you in my arms. I am hungry for you. Don't starve me now." He pulled her towards the sofa.

"No, not until you listen to me."

"What's so important that it can't wait? You know how many

times I had to beg my friend to let us use his apartment?"

"My parents are planning to marry me off as soon as I finish high school. I want to know, will you marry me?" Sito asked, holding his hand.

"You look more beautiful when you are angry." Kelly sang a Hindi film song. Sito wasn't impressed and kept pushing him away. For a moment, he seemed confused. Then he grabbed her again and said, "You are such a lovely thing, who else am I going to marry? Of course I'll marry you."

He was holding her in his strong arms and kissing her madly on her neck and nibbling on her ear. Kelly's kisses and the warmth of his body aroused her.

"Do you believe him?" asked Lucy, when Sito told her about what happened in the apartment.

"I don't know. Oh God, I wish I had been more careful." She felt depressed.

"Make sure he marries you now, kid," Lucy said. Then she too looked worried and added, "I knew this would happen. Well, you better take those pills carefully like I told you."

"I know he will marry me. We just have to figure out a way to get our parents talking to each other," Sito said in a low voice.

They continued to meet. She skipped classes to be with Kelly and stayed out late after school, making up all kinds of excuses to her parents. They spent much of their time in his friend's apartment. But Kelly also took her to Queen Elizabeth and Stanley Park and to English Bay and Spanish Banks. Sito was on top of the world.

Every time Sito wanted to discuss marriage, Kelly skillfully avoided the subject. It had become a routine. Mostly, they ended up in his friend's apartment. Sito was getting tired of this game. Each time she saw him she would cross the line, which is considered the most sinful in Punjabi culture.

During their last time together Sito refused to go to bed with him and insisted that he talk to his parents about them. He told her, "I'll talk to my parents when I feel like it. Stop this nonsense and get into the bed. If you don't want to, I can easily find someone else who will." Sito started to cry. Kelly grabbed her in his arms and said, "Oh, come here, you little baby, I was only kidding. Can't you see? Of course, I'll talk to my parents. Don't worry. I will take care of everything."

Then Kelly disappeared. She didn't see his car around. He didn't call her at home. Sito waited, her ears glued to the phone, expecting the phone to ring once, stop, and ring again after a few minutes.

A few days later, she was sitting in front of the TV, immersed in her sadness, when the phone rang. She looked at the clock. It was exactly the time Kelly called her on Saturdays. Her parents were out grocery shopping. At first, there was only one ring. In a few minutes, it rang again. Her heart jumped. She hurriedly lifted the receiver. But instead of Kelly's voice what she heard was sharp and unfamiliar. "So when are you coming to your favourite apartment to see me?" She was terrified and asked, "Who are you?"

"So now you are asking who I am? You had no fucking problem using my apartment whenever you wanted to, as if it belonged to your father." There was a pause. "I am Miki, Kelly's friend. Kelly has gone to India to get married. He left his car, and you, with me for safe-keeping while he is away. Now cut the bullshit and tell me, when are you coming to see me, to use your old familiar bed again?"

"I don't know who the hell you are! Don't ever call me again!" Sito slammed the receiver down. She held her head in her hands and fell on the sofa and stayed there motionless. Then she went into her room, got into her bed, and covered herself with the blanket. Her mother called out to her when she returned from the store. Sito said she had a headache and stayed in bed.

Later that evening she heard her mother and father talking about her marriage again. She put her hands to her ears and forced herself to go to sleep.

Today she had returned to school after many days. And now she had seen Miki in Kelly's car. In her fury she wanted to hurt him, break something. But she could only force herself to walk at a quick pace, not knowing where to go.

Fauji Banta Singh

I WAS DISAPPOINTED NOT TO SEE Banta Singh by the
stairs in front of his house where he always was, his aged
and slightly bent body supporting his weight on his cane.
I never saw him without that cane. Banta Singh was known as
Fauji, meaning soldier, even though he had retired from the
army a long time ago.

I was off work for ten weeks due to a foot injury. I thought
he might be sick or had gone to live with his younger son in
Williams Lake, as he had done two years ago. When I saw his
grandson, I asked him about Banta Singh. "Oh, he died a month
ago," he said without stopping or showing any emotion. I was
annoyed at his behaviour. Banta Singh had made my working
life colourful by simply being there.

I also knew his son Kartar Singh, and I went to his house the
same evening after work to give my condolences. Kartar Singh
was busy watching TV. His wife was in the kitchen preparing

dinner. Naseeb Kaur, the wife of Banta Singh, was sitting in a small sofa in one corner of the living room. With a string of beads in her hand, she was softly reciting Gurbani, the sacred Sikh scripture.

Kartar Singh and I exchanged a few customary words about Banta Singh and then there was complete silence. I was hoping to learn more about the circumstances of his death, and to ask Kartar Singh about Banta Singh's favourite walking stick, which he sometimes used as a stool to sit on. I wanted to have it to remember my friend, but I didn't have the nerve to ask Kartar Singh, and he seemed bored with my presence. I was ready to leave, when he said, "It was good to have him around the house and the hundred dollars that he paid for the little room."

I was sad for my friend Banta Singh. As I drove home, my mind was filled with many fond memories of him.

Rain or shine he would be outside the house waiting for me, as I came around after delivering mail on the street. He would be there even when it was snowing, which he hated with a passion. From September to April he wore a heavy blue jacket, with the hood showing its red lining underneath. In warm weather he would wear the old black suit he had brought from India years ago, or sometimes simply his khaki kurta and pajama. He had an elegant face made larger by his gray beard. It became a habit for me to spend a few minutes chatting with him each morning, no matter how late or rushed I was. I often found myself running to get to his house so I could talk to him.

Due to the dramatic increase in their numbers in Vancouver in the late sixties and early seventies, the Punjabis had become the target of racism from the local white community. In nineteen-seventy-one I was the only Punjabi postman in the area, and many white residents did not hide their prejudice. They would complain to my superiors if I was late a few minutes or let their dogs loose in their front yards. I would always look out for anything familiar. About twenty homes, out of the four hundred on my route, belonged to Punjabis. The smell of Punjabi cooking from these homes gave me a sense of intense belonging. I had special feelings about Banta Singh and his house because he was the only one who came out to talk to me. The other well-kept homes and tidy green lawns held no more charm for me than did the sawmill, where I had worked before the post office.

In his happier moods, Banta Singh would act like a child. Often he saluted me, using his right hand as he had done in the army, and he did this quite solemnly. One day he was holding his cane in his right hand and therefore used the left hand to salute. He presented an amusing picture and I couldn't control my laughter. To my pleasant surprise, he didn't mind and actually laughed with me. Later he would use this act to make me laugh.

One day he was holding a new stick in his hand, and his face was lit like that of a six-year-old excited by a new toy. The stick was actually an army field stool, its one end was sharp so it could push easily into the ground, and the other end opened up to make a small seat. He met me a few houses away from his home, happier than I had ever seen him. Pushing the sharp end into the ground he opened up the seat, sat on it with his legs opened wide and his hands on his knees. His white-bearded face glowed with joy.

Jerking his head up and down, he said to me, "What do you say now, Mister? Is this not the greatest thing in the world? This damn thing has been on my mind for the last fift y years. Our white officers used to have these, and they could sit anywhere with their asses supported comfortably, while we stood at full attention waiting for their orders. I finally found one in a downtown second-hand store yesterday."

One morning while I was still half a block away from his house, he came running towards me and said, "Saab-ji, Saab-ji, you are so late today. I have been waiting for more than an hour!" He called me by the honorific even though I had asked him repeatedly to call me by my name.

I looked at my watch, a little surprised, and said, "I am on time, not late at all; you sure seem to be in some kind of a rush today." I walked past him to deliver the mail next door. He looked restless standing there.

"What is the matter?" I called back.

"Since you are an educated person, I thought you would know whether what I've heard is true or not," he said, walking hurriedly to catch up with me.

"What have you heard?"

"This letter came from the government yesterday." He showed it to me and continued, "My grandson read it to me and he says that they are coming to check how much money I spend on food and shelter, and how much I have in the bank." He paused for a few seconds, then motioned to me to come closer to him where he was now standing on the sidewalk in front of his house.

In a secretive voice he said, "Son, I have some money in the bank. I thought that if there was any danger I could withdraw it and hide it somewhere else." There was fear on his face as he stood stiffly leaning over his cane, held firmly in both hands.

I didn't quite understand what he was trying to tell me, or the reason for his fear. To calm him down, I said, "Oh they are probably doing some kind of survey to raise pensions for you old-timers. Nobody will touch your money. Don't worry about it."

My response didn't satisfy him at all. Again in a secretive tone, which sounded quite comical, he said, "Son, you don't know about these white people, they must be thinking of stopping the pension for us immigrants. They know that we don't spend much money and they do not want to give us more than we need."

I started to laugh. He looked at me strangely as though I were deliberately being unreasonable. He said, with added seriousness and fear in his voice, "It is not a laughing matter, Saab-ji; it has happened to me once before. I used to be in a cavalry regiment in Patiala. Oh, it must have been around 1932, three years before I retired. We Indian soldiers used to save all our pay each month, and the white soldiers used to spend all theirs. The English commander thought, 'These Indians don't spend much, therefore they don't need any extra money.' Sure enough, they started to pay us less, and more to the white soldiers."

I was taken aback for a moment. Then I tried my best to reason with him that here in Canada no one can look at your bank balance, and even if you were to tell them how much you had, they could not touch your money. He calmed down a little, but the fear of losing his money and having his pension reduced persisted.

Banta Singh had served in the British Indian Army for sixteen years. Though it had been over thirty-five years since he retired, the way he talked and moved reflected his army training. This led to problems with other older Punjabis, who gathered in the local gurdwara, the Sikh temple, where Banta Singh went at least once a day. Most of them were village folks who had spent their lives working on family farms in Punjab. Banta Singh demanded special respect from them for being an ex-army man. On his part he became the butt of their collective ridicule for his snobbish attitude. Banta Singh would leave in frustration, muttering obscenities. He would continue to grumble until he arrived in his small basement room. I saw him on his way back from the gurdwara on one such occasion, and asked him, "Baba, you seem to be in a bit of a bad mood today! What happened?"

"These bloody old people, they are rotten. They sit in the home of God and aren't afraid of anything, but He watches all and will make them pay one day soon. God will cut out their dirty tongues soon enough." He kept muttering angrily, as he walked on home.

Later I asked Teja Singh, "Baba-ji, what happened today? Old Fauji Banta Singh was really mad."

Teja Singh, an old-time Canadian who always wore a small black turban, chuckled. "What could be the matter, young man? Banta Singh doesn't let anybody else talk once he starts his tales of army days. He was up to the same thing today. And you know the type of person Bishna is—a real dirty-minded old man. He said to Banta Singh, 'You think you are such a big shot and treat us like we are a bunch of village idiots. Now tell me, has your son ever allowed your old wife to come down to the basement to see you?' Banta Singh is very sensitive about this issue—he started to hurl names at Bishna and ran out of the place."

Teja Singh paused for a few seconds and added, "You know, all of these fellows get together and give the Fauji a hard time."

Banta Singh's marriage had not been going smoothly. He was extremely touchy about the subject and very bitter about his son's behaviour. He once told me, "This son of mine is a real maan choad, mother fucker. He has ordered his mother, the old woman, to stay upstairs and never to come down to the basement where I live. He takes and cashes her cheque every month and keeps the whole amount. The poor soul sits in a chair chanting Gurbani all day. I also used to hand him my entire cheque, which allowed me to sit at the table and eat my roti with the rest of the family. Now since I give him only a hundred dollars a month, he is always angry with me. He sends my roti downstairs. I used to be able to sit in the bathtub upstairs once in a while. Now I can only take a shower if I get a chance at the right moment, since he has rented out the bigger part of the basement to white people. He owns two other homes in the city. I don't know what he is going to do with all this money."

Banta Singh had lived with his younger son in Williams Lake for a few years. He couldn't get along with his daughter-in-law there and came to live with the older son in Vancouver. When he saw me delivering mail on his street the first time, he didn't speak to me right away. For a couple of days he just watched me from a distance. Then one day while I was climbing down the stairs of his house, after delivering the mail, he hesitantly acknowledged me with a slight movement of his head, and then said hello in English in a low, unsure voice.

Understanding his dilemma, I smiled and said in a loud voice, "Baba-ji ki haal ai, how are you?" He was overjoyed. He came towards me, energetically shook my hand, and kept on shaking it. He tapped my shoulder happily and said, "I thought you were probably from Fiji or something. But you are really one of our own—this is great. Where is your village back home?"

"Baba-ji, my village is close to Jalandhar," I told him, staring straight at him, wanting to know his reaction because I knew that he belonged to a different region of the Punjab. He seemed a bit disappointed, as I expected. Then suddenly he became cheerful again and exclaimed, "It doesn't matter, and it is all the same in a foreign land anyway."

We became instant friends, forgetting the big difference in our ages. Each day we met and talked about everything from the politics of India to the younger generations of Punjabis growing up here. He told me stories about the Punjabi people of his own age group who played cards in the local park. He knew all the important people and the inside politics of the Ross Street gurdwara, which was close to his house. It was considered the most important religious place for the Sikhs in the entire country. Its management had ongoing internal conflicts, which often evolved into open fights. Banta Singh recounted these fights in detail and cursed the leaders for their conduct. He seemed genuinely concerned about the damage that was being done to the reputation of his Sikh religion.

He had become terribly upset when he found out that Vancouver's oldest gurdwara, on 2nd Avenue, had been sold to build a new one on Ross Street. "Saab-ji, only God can save a community that cannot look after the important places where their forefathers have made history. I can't understand how these idiots think. Do they have no sense, no shame?" That was the first religious place built in North America by the Sikhs, in 1907.

Once, in a very secretive tone, he invited me to come to the gurdwara. "Son, you must come to the guru-ghar this weekend." I thought there must be a wedding in the family, or perhaps his family had initiated an akhandpath, the religious service. Just to make sure, I asked him, "Is your family doing something special on the weekend, Baba-ji?"

"No, it is not a family matter, it's much more important. You must come."

When I asked again, he looked around suspiciously and said, "There is a big election on Sunday. It is rumored that the communists are trying to take over the gurdwara. We must never let them take over the home of the Guru."

"Aren't you always criticizing the leadership? Now let there be a change this time," I said.

"Son, I know that these leaders aren't ideal people, and one day they will surely suffer for their ill deeds, but at least they have faith in the Guru Granth Sahib, while these communists don't even believe in God. They will turn the gurdwara into their political headquarters."

I felt like arguing with him, but looking at his sincere face, I decided to keep quiet.

At times Banta Singh irritated me by his pretentious tone and high tales of his army days. Reacting to his boastfulness one day, I said, "Baba, when the British massacred Punjabis in Amritsar in 1919, you were in the army; when they massacred the Sikhs during the Jaiton Morcha, you were in the army; when they hanged Bhagat Singh, you were in the army."

He stood there, hurt and speechless at my sudden turn-around. Feeling guilty, I quickly changed the topic. After that, though, he never talked about his army days in the same tone with me.

He often complained about members of his family. He disliked the way his grandchildren behaved. One day his fourteen-year old grandson walked by us while we stood chatting. Looking at his long flowing hair, Banta Singh said with displeasure in his voice, "Look at him. Look how he has grown his hair, and the style of his clothes, isn't he a disgrace? He could be straightened out in a minute with a strap, but it is a totally different game here, in this country." In his voice, there was a sense of real loss and defeat.

His loneliness became much more pronounced when he talked about his wife. "As long as I was in the army, she used to be happy with me; especially when I came home on my annual two-month leave. That is when we had our kids—two boys and a girl. Since then, she has never spoken to me properly or shown any affection towards me. Now we live here in the same house, but she never speaks to me. She recites Gurbani twenty-four hours a day. I sometimes wonder what sins she might have committed that she needs to do this." He spoke about his wife as if he were talking about a total stranger.

One day I met him as he was returning from someone's home after a ritual reading of the Guru Granth Sahib. He looked very tired, which was a bit unusual because he was always upbeat after reading the Gurbani. He said to me, "Son, I feel so home-sick these days, here in this foreign land. I often wish that when I open my eyes in the morning I could get up in my village. Life was not so bad there in the fields, spending time with people that I had grown up with. I never felt like this even in the army when I was away from home for so long." I could see in his eyes his burning desire to go back to the village, and mused about the love a birthplace holds for people.

"Go then, for a while; the airfare is cheap these days."

"I really would like to, but you have no idea of my situation, and the enmity I face from relatives. Everyone will cast an evil eye on my money. You never know, some idiot could simply finish me off in order to rob me. You can't trust people any-more. With God's will, I am going to spend the rest of my days in this land now."

To cheer him up, I said, "How about if we find a white woman for you to have a good time with, Baba-ji?" Spontaneously, that childlike smile spread on his face. Almost blushing he said, "No sonny, why become sinners at this age? Just a few more years are left now and I will spend them singing the name of almighty God."

After a short pause he said, "Sometimes I do feel the desire to experience the touch of white skin at least once in my life-time. You know, this country is really awful that way—it is so hard for a person to remain pious. Nobody hides anything. I just returned from reading the Guru Granth at Karnail Singh's house. His youngest son got married a couple of weeks ago—the bastard kept making noises with his wife in the next room. You know how thin the walls are in these homes. It is hard not to have sinful thoughts, even while one is reciting the sacred text—forgive me, my dear God." He looked up to the sky as he always did when addressing God.

We both understood that we were only kidding; still he seemed to have enjoyed my suggestion. He said, "Come over to my basement after work sometime and we will have a drink or two, and I'll tell you some stories of my younger days. I have not only saluted the English; I have done some wild things too, you know."

I accepted his invitation. I wanted to listen to his stories and see his small room in the basement, but I injured myself that week and our plan for a party never materialized.

Banta Singh did everything in his life that a normal Indian person is supposed to do. He worked hard all his life to raise his children. In old age, he fulfilled his religious duties by reciting the holy book countless times and praying for the well-being of his children and grandchildren. Now he was gone. I was filled with a strange sadness for my friend Fauji Banta Singh.

The Burden

D URING KIRPAL'S LAST VISIT to the village, his uncle
came over to his house and begged him for help. The
two families had had nothing to do with each other
for years because of an ongoing feud over the division of family land. Twenty years ago, after Kirpal finished high school,
he married a girl from Canada. A few years later he moved to
Canada with his whole family, while his uncle remained in the
village, living in extreme poverty. He had two daughters and an
eight-year-old son. The oldest daughter, Resho, had just turned
sixteen.

Out of sympathy, Kirpal promised his uncle that he would
find a husband for Resho and bring her over to Canada. However, he would have to convince his mother and younger brother
Joga. Joga said very little but his mother was not happy. She
said, "Kirpal, have you already forgotten that when your father
died five years ago, your uncle didn't even have the decency
to send his condolences?" Kirpal had already thought of an
answer to that. "Mother, we know what kind of a person he is,
but must we also behave the same way? After all, they are our

family and they need help."

Convincing his mother and brother was easier than finding a boy for Resho. Kirpal spoke to relatives and friends, with no luck. A year had passed since his promise and he was getting worried. Desperate, he chose a man he knew his family would not like.

Kirpal had to figure out a way to convince his mother and brother about his choice. One Saturday evening, the two brothers were having a few drinks before dinner. The kids were playing in the family room by the kitchen and the women were busy making dinner. Their mother came into the living room to sit with them. Kirpal poured himself another scotch, settled back on the sofa, and said, "I have somebody in mind for Resho, but I'm not sure you will like him." He saw Joga's face become tense and thought of leaving the matter for some other time. Then he looked at his mother and continued, "Both of you know the guy. Yes, he has some bad habits, but he is basically a good man. You can count on him to stick with you in any situation. Just last week, I ran into him in the beer parlour on Hastings Street. There were four of us and the guy wouldn't let us buy even one round of beer. He—"

Joga banged his glass on the table and said, "Are you crazy? You want to ruin your own cousin's life by marrying her to that jerk?"

"Who are you talking about, Kirpal?" his mother asked.

"He worked in our mill and was fired because he was drunk most of the time," said Joga.

"It's not Gian Kaur's brother, what's his name, Jarnail, is it?" said Mother, sitting down. "No, for God's sake we don't want to commit a sin. He is no man. Drunk twenty-four hours a day. He was dead drunk when he had the accident that killed his first wife."

Kirpal said, looking directly at his mother, "Bibi, there are hundreds of accidents everyday. These kinds of things happen according to one's karma anyway. You remember Dalip Singh, who used to live in my brother-in-law's basement, his whole family died in an accident—he himself, his wife, and their son. He was driving and he had never even smelled liquor in his life."

Mother fell silent. After a brief pause Kirpal added, "I know Jarnail is a good man. He owns a house, which he rents out. He had a permanent job and will probably find another one soon, since he has so many friends everywhere."

Joga said, "People like Jarnail never change. His sister managed his money when he lived with her and bought that house for him. Have you ever seen his face in daylight? He has so many scars from fights, his face looks like a map of some old Indian city. No, brother, I don't agree with you. Just imagine, Resho is still a child, tender and beautiful like a rose."

"What about the promise we made to Uncle?" asked Kirpal.

"You made the promise. I guess you wanted to be a big shot," Joga said.

Mother looked at Joga and said, "Son, your brother did that out of duty. In times of need, it's only your own kin that comes to help. The most worthy thing a man can do in his lifetime is to take care of his daughter or sister. Since you have no sister of your own, marrying off your cousin is your duty. Maybe one day Resho will be able to bring her folks over to Canada and it will change their fate as well."

She walked over to Kirpal, placed a hand on his shoulder and said, "If Kirpal Singh—may God grant my son a long life—has promised to arrange the marriage of his cousin, both of you are equally responsible now. Find someone better than Jarnail if you can, but you must do your duty."

Joga was silent. "My sons always obey me," Mother thought to herself. "People back in the village will respect me for helping my dead husband's brother and his family."

They did not talk about it again. Kirpal took care of everything on his own. He invited Jarnail's sister to meet with his mother one day while Joga was out with his family. He took Jarnail to the immigration department and filled out the sponsorship forms.

"Resho is arriving on Saturday," Kirpal said to his brother. "Jarnail's sister, Gian Kaur, will also come with us to the airport."

The news came as a total shock to Joga. Seeing no reaction from his mother, Joga realized that he was the only one who didn't like this arranged marriage of his cousin. Unable to control his anger, he got up and left the room.

Joga thought about this the next few days and decided to keep quiet. Their family was well respected for maintaining harmony among the large numbers of relatives, friends, and acquaintances in the Vancouver area. Joga didn't want to harm the image and disrupt the unity of his family.

Most of their relatives and friends expressed shock at the news of Resho's arranged marriage to Jarnail. Those who resented Kirpal's family were secretly happy that he was not able to find a more decent match for his cousin. Others imagined a rift developing between Joga and Kirpal, which gave them vicarious satisfaction. Some even believed that Kirpal had intentionally meant to hurt his uncle. Nobody considered opposing the marriage of a young girl to a much older man and a known alcoholic. Instead they all expressed agreement, saying, "Oh, Jarnail will be fine, once he is married."

Relatives and friends of both families, numbering in the hundreds, were waiting for Jarnail at the gurdwara on the morning of his wedding. He arrived more than an hour late. He had been drinking with friends, and had had only a couple of hours of sleep when Gian Kaur forced him out of bed. The minute he got up, he poured himself a drink.

Going around the Guru Granth Sahib four times, the most reverent part of a Sikh marriage ceremony, Jarnail was unable to walk straight. Wrapped in the red wedding suit, Resho seemed devoid of life, and only moved forward when helped by her cousins. Joga watched Jarnail with disgust, but kept his cool as demanded by the situation. No one else witnessing the unusual scene in the gurdwara uttered a word of protest.

After the ceremony there was the midday meal in the gurdwara. Jarnail spilled food all over the table. Joga was ready to say something to him when his mother came over and asked him to go help in the kitchen.

Though smoking and drinking are strictly prohibited in and around a Sikh gurdwara, Jarnail still lit a cigarette and asked his friend Bahadar to pour him a drink as they stood by their car in the parking lot. Gian Kaur and the other women brought Resho out and seated her in the car. They were going to a local park to have pictures taken.

Seated in the back, Jarnail only spoke with his friend Bahadar, who was driving the car, ignoring Resho sitting beside him. Gian Kaur sat silently in the front seat, careful not to say anything that might provoke Jarnail to behave even more foolishly.

When they arrived in the park, Gian Kaur got out and opened the rear door to help Resho. She straightened Resho's suit and the chunny on her head. They stood awkwardly near a bench and silently waited for Jarnail to join them. After a few minutes Gian Kaur went back to the car and saw Jarnail with a glass in his hand. She pleaded, "Jarnail, please don't drink any more now. We have to go to Kirpal's house and there will be lots of people there. You can drink all you want tonight."

"Oh, come on, Sis, this is my big day. I should be allowed to do whatever I want."

He started to pour a drink. She grabbed the glass from his hand. "Stop wasting time, get out, and pose for the pictures. We are already late."

"The hell with you and your pictures, I am not getting out or posing for anyone," Jarnail said angrily. The hired photographer who had followed them in his own car watched them, baffled. Finally, Bahadar coaxed Jarnail to come out of the car, but before posing for pictures, he insisted that Bahadar be allowed to stand with him for every shot.

Jarnail was the first one out of the car when they arrived at Kirpal's house. He staggered and finished his cigarette with long, gulping puffs. Kirpal's wife Surinder and the other women escorted Resho into the house. It was full of people, but was missing the lively laughter, noise and singing heard during a typical Punjabi wedding. Joga was by the door as Resho walked in. Her face was pale and lifeless. Joga felt as though he had blood on his hands. I should have stopped Kirpal from doing this, he thought.

Joga forced a smile when he shook Jarnail's hand. He led him towards the side of the house near the door to the basement. Jarnail suddenly stopped and said, "Are you going to make me sit in the basement? I am your sister's husband and you are my sala, brother-in-law, now. You have to give me the respect a sister's husband deserves."

Joga stood there with clenched fists. Any other time he would have killed a man for saying sala to him. The other guests, all men, who had stood up on the arrival of the groom, held their breath, expecting something unpleasant to occur. Luckily,

Kirpal stepped in. He embraced Jarnail and said to the others, "Now that our brother Jarnail is here, let's have a drink, everyone."

The guests sat back in their seats. It was a large room with sofas and chairs set in a semicircle. Bottles of scotch, Canadian whisky, and rum were placed on two rectangular tables in the middle of the room. Jarnail poured himself a large drink of scotch as soon as he sat down.

No one spoke for a while and the tension in the room was becoming unbearable. An elderly man in a gray suit said, "So Jarnail Singh, do you hear from your father back home? Is he doing okay? I have known him for a long time, he is a very gentle person, your father."

Jarnail washed down the scotch and made a sour face. "Uncle, I don't send him money anymore so I don't hear from him, end of story."

A few people in the room laughed nervously while others gazed at their watches. Jarnail looked around the room and saw an old acquaintance. "Gurmit, my old friend, what the hell are you doing here? Come and have a drink with me. Hey, you remember when we picked up that hooker from Hastings Street? Man, did we have some fun that night. Come and have a drink with me." Gurmit sat frozen. He was thankful when someone else attracted Jarnail's attention.

Kirpal, meantime, had gone upstairs. He called out to his wife, "Surinder, hurry up and get the bride ready for vidaygee, the sending off ceremony, as soon as you can."

A middle-aged woman, who was Kirpal's maternal aunt, said, "Kirpal, the women want to invite the groom upstairs to do some traditional stuff and the girls want to cut the cake as well."

"Never mind the cake and the bloody traditions. Hurry up

and get Resho ready to go," said Kirpal on his way back to the basement.

The women brought Resho out, and the men came up from the basement. They all stood quietly on the front lawn near the groom's car. A few of the white neighbours also came out of their homes to watch the Indian wedding rituals and admire the colourful Punjabi suits worn by the women.

Traditionally, Punjabi women cry when the bride finally leaves her parents' home, which is the only instance of dramatic emotion in an otherwise happy affair. However, when saying goodbye to Resho, some women were actually sobbing with grief. Before getting into the car, Resho cried on the shoulders of Joga and her aunt, as if she was never going to see them again.

Bahadar was helping Jarnail to the car; he was too drunk to walk by himself. Gian Kaur sat in the front seat and fixed her gaze on the street. The women helped Resho into the back seat and Bahadar pushed Jarnail in from the other side. The car moved slowly and then raced away.

Joga could not control himself anymore. He said to Kirpal, "Are you satisfied now, brother, with that fucking asshole as the husband of our sister?"

"Look! We don't have to put up with his nonsense. It is only a distant relationship. If he behaves, we will socialize with him; if not, we won't bother. The main thing is that we have to be thankful to God that our responsibility, the weight from our shoulders, has been taken off."

My First Memory

THE VERY FIRST MEMORY of my life is about fear. In fact, fear is connected with every recollection of my childhood. Ever since my mother warned me about the bhabhoos— a big heavy word for little ants—from that moment on I have been scared of everything, especially things that crawl.

As an Indian, I understand better than anyone else the importance and significance of fear in one's life. The great traditions of making children know fear from the beginning sets people of my native country apart. I'll have more to say about this grand philosophical tradition of raising young ones in our country. For now, let me continue to tell you the unforgettable very first memory of my childhood.

I was very young, maybe two or three years old at the most. Now you may ask: how can I remember something from such an early age? Dear reader-ji, there are things one remembers no matter from how long ago, especially someone as important and famous as myself.

Anyway, it was a dark night. We were sleeping in our two-and-a-half-bed-wide dalaan, the big room. Due to some new fear I had picked up during the day, I was unable to sleep. I was afraid and crying constantly. My father wanted to have some important secret talk with my mother, as he usually did at night. Once or twice my mother tried to reassure me and urged me to go to sleep.

I tried my best to sleep. But uncontrollably I would start again, "Mom, I am afraid, I want to sleep with you."

My father was patient with me for a while. Then he thought it was time to teach me to behave.

So as a knowledgeable, caring father, he came close to my little cot and said in a sensible fatherly voice, "You sister-fucker, dirty son of a whore, are you going to sleep quietly or not? If I hear one more peep out of you, I am going to give you a lesson you will never forget in your entire life."

He left, and just as he started his important and secret business with my mom, I began to cry again.

My father immediately got up and came to my side. His beard, his chest, hair and the long dark hair on his head made him look like a monster. I became even more afraid and unable to stop crying.

He lifted me by my armpits and stood me down on the floor beside the cot. Then he roared in his full voice, "You mother-fucker; I'll show you how to cry. You haven't cried yet, you will cry now!" He slapped me hard with all his strength. I fell, hitting my head on the bed's leg. My mother ran to my side but father stopped her.

After father went to bed, mother picked me up from the floor. She never told me if I was unconscious from the blow. Years later she told me that I was sick for a whole month. After that night something changed in me forever. Out of fear, I would

32

not go near my father.

As far as I can remember, I was afraid of my father till the day I became strong enough to make him fear me.

I had learned the most valuable lesson: Whenever and however possible, make people fear you.

The Broken Window

AFTER THE WEATHERMAN HAD FINISHED the forecast, Harnam Singh switched the TV off. Daya Kaur slowly stood up, supporting herself with her hands on her knees, and went straight to her bed. She knew that her husband would take a few more minutes to come to the bedroom.

Harnam Singh walked up to the large window of the living room, lifted the side of the curtain, and looked out at the tranquil street. It had been raining all day. Even now, a slow drizzle was visible under the street lights. It was the middle of October and the nights were cold. The old couple lived on a quiet street in East Vancouver. There was hardly any traffic at night. The tall lamp posts stood still, all by themselves, as though having taken a vow of silence.

Harnam Singh stood by the window for a few seconds, scrutinizing the houses across the street. Then he went into the washroom; he cleared his throat and nostrils, making loud noises. He made them deliberately, as though to frighten away the still ness in the house. After he had got into bed and switched the small table lamp off, Daya Kaur complained in her usual manner, "Sleep doesn't come easily to old people."

Harnam Singh adjusted his pillow in silence. Daya Kaur spoke again, "It was so nice to have the Gill family in the basement. At night, their child got up and cried, and the house sounded so alive."

Harnam Singh took a deep sigh and thought about the Gills, which he didn't like to do, but Daya Kaur reminded him every night. They had rented out the place mainly to feel less lonely, but the extra money came in handy to buy special gifts for their own grandchildren. However, it was an illegal suite, a jealous neighbour had complained, and the city forced the Gills out.

After a long while, just to break the stillness, he asked, "How long did they stay in our basement?"

"For two and a half years. Their son Gurmail was only six months old when they moved in during the summer of 1973. And the little girl Ruby was born a year later in '74." Daya Kaur was very fond of remembering and repeating dates. She remembered the day she left her village to come to Canada and the exact date and time she landed in Vancouver's small airport at the time.

"They were such lovely children. The girl looked exactly like our Sunita when she was born," said Harnam Singh.

Silence again.

They both thought about their children—a son and a daughter—now married and living in their own homes. Their son Dave, soon after getting married, moved to Toronto where he found a job with the Immigration Department. He visited them once or twice a year. Their daughter Sunita lived in Richmond with her husband and two children, and came to see them once a week. She and the grandchildren were the centre of their lives. Harnam Singh had retired from the sawmill where he had worked for more than twenty-five years as a green-chain-puller. For a few summers after retirement he had worked in the Fraser Valley farms; now he was too old to work.

He yawned and said waheguru, looking up into the darkness. The words of prayer came out of his mouth spontaneously, without his permission or wish. Daya Kaur turned on her side and said it almost the same way as her husband, "True God, have mercy on all."

Having said these words, they silently waited for sleep. The house was serene and the only sound came from their old refrigerator that rumbled when the motor stopped, and droned when it started again.

They were both lying awake when they heard a crash of shattering glass followed by a heavy thud on their living-room floor. The sharp echos of the shards hitting the hardwood floor pierced through the stillness of the night. They jumped with fright but knew exactly what had happened and were filled with anger. This was not the first time their window had been broken at night.

Harnam Singh, weak and shaken, got up, picked up the small stick that he kept by his bed, and started towards the door. Daya Kaur tried to stop him. "Dave's Dad, have you gone mad? We don't have the strength to stand up straight; how can we fight these devils? They could throw another rock and hurt us. Don't go into the living room. Let's go to the kitchen and call the police."

Harnam Singh, shaking with anger, said, "What is the use of calling the police? Have we not done so twice already this month? First time they came and asked us a whole bunch of useless questions and went away looking at us as if we were the trouble makers. The second time they didn't even come for two hours."

Together they walked to the kitchen and found the old cardboard on which they had written a few phone numbers. Harnam Singh dialed a number. A tired and hostile voice answered the phone, took his name and address, and promised to send help.

Daya Kaur went into the living room and lifted the curtain a little to look out. The street was as quiet as it was before they had gone to bed. She watched the homes on both sides of the street and saw no movement of any kind. "Surely they must have heard the sound of the window breaking," she thought, and felt lonely and scared. Momentarily, her mind travelled back to her village in the Punjab. "The whole neighbourhood would come to help in time of need," she said to herself.

Then she remembered their neighbours George and Bernice. "If they were still living here they would definitely come out to help us." George and Bernice had been the nicest couple on the street. George had lived in India for a few years just before the Second World War, and later moved to Canada from his native England. A sudden heart attack killed him a year ago and Bernice moved to an apartment a few months later.

With these thoughts running through her head, Daya Kaur went and stood by her husband, who was mutely observing the broken pieces of glass on the living room floor. Then he too went to the window and stared out into the street. He knew that the culprits would have fled in seconds and there would be no one around. Still, he looked into the motionless street with an empty look in his eyes, not trying to see anything at all. He turned around, took a few heavy steps back, and slumped into the armchair.

Daya Kaur found the silence unbearable and started to mumble. "May God punish these devils. What have we done to them that they are hurting us like this? We have lived on this street for so long and have never said a harsh word to anyone . . . "

Harnam Singh interrupted her. "Why do you always go on talking like this. Who are you trying to tell all this to? These monkeys do not have enough sense to understand anything. They just like to amuse themselves by terrorizing old people after a few beers."

"Is this some kind of new beer that they drink now? People have always had beer and nobody has ever done this kind of thing to us in the past," retorted Daya Kaur.

Harnam Singh got up once again, looked out the window, and returned, cursing the police. "These bastards take their sweet time don't they?"

"What could they do anyway? Who knows how many places they have to visit each night."

"Why don't you keep quiet, you seem to have a lot of sympathy for the cops." Harnam Singh was at a loss what to do. If Daya Kaur had not been saying something, he probably would have, since the stillness was eating away at him too.

After a couple of minutes, Daya Kaur spoke again, "I was saying that maybe we should call Sunita and her husband . . . "

Harnam Singh again interrupted her with, "What could they do in the middle of the night? Besides, they both have to go to work early in the morning."

They remained silent for a while. Then Daya Kaur started again, "I believe that the real reasons behind this window-breaking and calling us Hindus and Pakis on the street are these newcomers, these visitors. The young people who come straight from villages in Punjab have no idea how to live in a big city and to behave properly. Their stupid behaviour is creating all these problems for everybody. We have lived here for so long and never before has any white man treated us like this."

This time Harnam Singh didn't interrupt her and she fell

silent looking at him.

He was also trying to figure out why this was happening. Some workers in his mill had often talked about racism but he never paid any attention; it was something that was just there, part of life, no more no less. Like many other Punjabi workers, he thought it was the privilege of the white people to look down upon them. "We would never let the low-caste chamaar or chuhrra come near our kitchen back in the village," he would say, justifying the white people's right to discriminate.

But Harnam Singh couldn't understand why he was being victimized this way now. He considered himself a god-fearing and law-abiding man. He had always kept out of other people's ways. After much thinking, he came to the same conclusion as Daya Kaur; all this was because of the large number of newly arrived young people from Punjab. They entered the country as visitors and tried to become permanent immigrants by any means possible.

Then he remembered the last time their window was broken. Some young Punjabis had come to see him afterwards. They sat discussing the issues of racial hatred, politics, and the ups and downs of the economy, all of which he found strange. After they left, he had said to Daya Kaur, "These young people make no sense at all. Now that they have started to eat three full meals everyday, they think they already own this land. Can you believe it, they were saying that it was the police and the government that was directly responsible for these attacks on poor people like us. Listen to these new, educated ones, eh!"

Harnam Singh was drowned in his thoughts. Daya Kaur repeated what she had said just a couple of minutes earlier, "Dave's Dad, phone them again. No one has come yet."

He was irritated even more. He knew that when the police came, it wouldn't make any difference. There was nothing else to do except wait.

The silence was agonizing. Daya Kaur started another of her tales, "When I went to the bank yesterday, there were dozens of policemen around. There must have been six or seven police cars with lights flashing. They had locked all the doors of the bank. The police were running back and forth with their pistols in their hands. Then after a while, everything was quiet. They opened all the doors. The cops went back to their cars chatting leisurely. A couple of them stood inside the bank, talking and laughing with that shameless, red-haired hussy who answers phone calls sitting at the table doing absolutely nothing all day long. I asked the teller what happened. She said that someone pushed the alarm button by mistake."

Harnam Singh heard Daya Kaur's story. He was angry. Those young Punjabis were saying precisely the same thing, he thought. Their exact words came to mind, "The government is there to protect the rich; they do not care about the average person."

He also remembered what his friend Mohan Singh had told him the other day: "The gurdwara committee people caught a few young white hooligans who were harassing worshippers on their way to the gurdwara, and handed them to the police. The police let them go free right in front of the gurdwara and nobody could say a thing." Harnam Singh grew angrier as he remembered that.

They heard a car stop in front of their house. They waited for what seemed like a long time, then finally there was knocking on the door. Two white officers came into the house. They took off their hats and held them in their hands. One officer started to question them: "What time was the window broken? . . . who were they? . . . did you see anyone? . . . what were you doing at the time? . . . do you know anyone who would want to break your window?" He was taking notes in his small notebook as he spoke to them. The second cop looked aimlessly behind the curtains and under the sofa. With his huge black boots, he tipped over the rock that was still lying in the middle of the room. After a while, they left. On their way out the officer with the notebook said, "We are sorry for your troubles. We will try and find out who broke the window. In the meantime, call your insurance company and have the glass replaced."

Harnam Singh hurriedly closed the door behind them, as though he was afraid they might come back in.

Off Track

I CAN'T SLEEP. IF I CLOSE my eyes, the same terrible scene
haunts me. The memory tortures me. The doctor says that
the effects of such incidents last for a long time.

The old woman who lives in the neighbourhood, the one my
mom calls Maasy, is the only one who comes to our home these
days. Just like my mother, she worries about me when she sees
me sitting home all alone watching TV or reading a book. She
thinks I should be going out with friends or playing some kind
of sport or something. She's just come from India. My mom
started calling her Maasy from the moment she met her. "She is
every bit like my own mother," said my mom. My sister Reshi
and I call her Maan-ji. Maan-ji doesn't know about our terrible past, and there is no one else who knows us here. That was
the reason why we left Toronto; it was impossible to live where
people knew what had happened to us.

No one knows anything about us here in Vancouver except
Maan-ji. She seems to love us so much that it wouldn't matter

even if she was aware of the incident. She is different from the Punjabi women we knew in Toronto. She doesn't ask many questions. Sometimes she comes and sits quietly with us, and at other times she talks a lot and says nice, comforting things in her own unique way. She often starts with, "The elders have said," and then she will add some old proverb. I don't always fully understand her; still, I find her soothing. One day she said to me, "Deesh, son, never be discouraged in life. The elders have said, the rains are only pleasant to those who have suffered from the drought." Then the other day she said, "Never expect somebody else to help you; the elders have said, O brave man, swim with the strength of your own arms."

I'm beginning to have the same feelings of love and trust for her as I have for my mom. She is the only person besides my mom who is concerned about me. Just yesterday, I heard her say to Mom, "Nimmi, dhiey, daughter, your son worries too much, he should be playing and running around like other boys his age." Mom didn't reply. Most of the time she just sits still, depressed and pensive.

I'm like her. After work I don't go anywhere except to visit the nearby library once in a while. I have read all the Punjabi novels there. I have started reading English books now. I don't understand much, but that doesn't seem to make any difference. I read to keep busy. Lately, when I can't sleep and get tired of watching TV, I write in this notebook, as I'm doing now.

Mom has been even more depressed lately. Something else happened earlier today that made her cry. I often quarrel with Reshi, but I have never hit her as violently as I did this morning. I don't know why, I suddenly became irritated with her. I started hitting her like someone gone mad. Mom was crying and trying to protect Reshi from me. "Stop it," she said, "I know you are angry. We are all angry. But hitting your sister is not going to solve anything." I regret my actions now. But I don't know what happened. I was hitting her as if I was going to kill her.

Afterwards, when Maan-ji came over, she talked to me for a long time. She said, "Deesh, son, you are the only hope for your poor mother and your sister. Your duty is to protect them."

I want to see the same beautiful and cheerful face of my mom that I see in the picture on our television set in the living room. I am sitting between Mom and Dad, leaning towards Dad with my right hand resting on Mom's knee. I was seven and this was the first time I had ever worn a two-piece suit. Reshi, only a few months old, is sitting in my mom's lap. This is a picture of a family that will never be together again.

My mom's sorrow is permanent. Even Reshi never speaks loudly or laughs at home. I don't know how she behaves in school with her friends. Maybe she will learn to enjoy life in school; I was never able to do that. I'm simply relieved I don't have to go to school anymore. I was new from India, physically weak and tiny-looking. Everyone in class laughed at my poor English.

At school, the Punjabi boys, especially, taunted me, calling me Deeshi, the feminine version of my name. What could I do? How could I fight them all? So I kept quiet all the time. And when the terrible incident took place, they began to make fun of me openly. Since the news was in the English newspapers, the non-Punjabis also found out that I was the son of a murderer. I simply became quieter. And the muter I became, the more troubled I was inside.

I had learned to be this way even before I came to Canada. This was when we lived in Agra, a city far away from our village in Punjab. Mom used to say, "You always sit quietly like your father, it is not good."

44

I wasn't always like that. I was active, mischievous, happy, and carefree like my friends in the village. Then things changed. Soon after the attack on the Golden Temple in Amritsar, the police came to arrest my father on suspicion of terrorist activity against the government. He hid from them and in the village the rumour started that he had joined the Sikh extremists. The police would come and harass my mom and my grandfather. Finally, my grandfather decided to take us away from the village to go live with some distant relatives in Agra for safety.

Life in the city was completely different from that in my village. The school I went to was so much larger. Some of the teachers were friendly towards me, but I had difficulty understanding and speaking Hindi. I was always afraid at school and on the streets because I wore a turban. Only two or three other students wore turbans in the entire school. When we heard about the attacks on the Sikhs in Delhi and other cities after Prime Minister Indira Gandhi's assassination by her two Sikh bodyguards, we were terrified. My mom hated Indira Gandhi with a passion. She blamed her for all the problems we were going through. She believed Mrs Gandhi created the situation that eventually led to the attack on Amritsar. Had these events not taken place, we would have lived a normal life in our own home in the village. Now that she was dead, Mom was even more afraid.

After school, I mostly stayed inside our small house. Occasionally, I would go to visit a friend who lived nearby. His name was Narinder and he also wore a turban. When I was with Narinder, Mom didn't worry so much. One day on our way back from school, we were hassled by a group of kids. I was scared but Narinder didn't show any fear. When Mom heard about it, she was alarmed. From then on, she stopped worrying only when I was safely home. In Agra, we passed our days this way, in constant fear.

Grandfather came to visit us from time to time. Our relatives had strictly forbidden my father from visiting them because they didn't want to get into any trouble with the police. One day Grandfather came to see us and he took Mom away with him. When she came back after two days, I saw a faint smile on her face. It had been a long time since I had seen her smile. She told me secretly that my dad had left the country and gone abroad and soon he would send for us. She didn't want our relatives to know about it. This bit of news didn't bring any immediate change in our daily lives, but it brought us new hope. We began to spend our days with the dream of a bright future and faced our day-to-day difficulties with a new strength.

There was no end to our wait. Four years passed. We regularly received letters from Dad and a few times some money as well. Mom would read Dad's letters first and then she would let me read them. She would reply to him herself, only once in a while asking me to write. Dad told us that he had first secretly entered Germany with a group of other Punjabis, and after a long wait they were able to hide in a ship's cargo and stow away to Canada. He had applied for refugee status in Canada, but the authorities were taking a long time to decide his case.

Dad's letters were always filled with encouraging words. In reply, we would ask him not to worry about us, though actually our relatives were tired of us and wanted us to leave. They took for themselves most of the money that came from my father. We didn't really care about our problems; we just wanted to get out of there and go to Canada. We felt like we were waiting on a platform of a railway station, paying no attention to the crowds, the noise, the pushing and shoving all around us. The train would arrive any minute to take us away from all that madness and we would be on our way to heaven.

Mom, Reshi, and I slept on one cot. At night Mom often talked about the good life in the village and told us many things about our dad. He was a deeply religious man and was respected by the villagers. Even though he had owned only a few acres of land, he had worked hard and been planning to buy a tractor. She told us how much he loved all three of us. Not only us, he loved everybody. But the attack on the Golden Temple by the army saddened him profoundly. He often went to the village gurdwara and sat there by himself for long periods. Someone from the village reported this to the police and he was suspected of being an extremist. There were at the time several terrorist attacks in retaliation against the assault on the Golden Temple. Mom said that Dad was a very kind man who would never hit even a stray dog. He could not be a terrorist. After listening to Mom, I believed there was no person better than my father; others appeared small and insignificant in comparison. I was proud of him and longed to be with him.

Finally, one fine morning, we arrived in Toronto. Dad came to meet us at the airport. He embraced us each in turn. In a new place among strange people, I felt secure and happy in my father's strong arms. Nothing else mattered.

We drove home from the airport, Reshi and I sitting in the back. It was a big red car. I had never seen the inside of such a car before. While Reshi was busy watching tall buildings and cars on the road, I secretly glanced at my father. I thought he was the most handsome man on earth. I realized, though, that I had imagined him to be a lot bigger and stronger. Mom had created such a picture of him.

Our home was a small apartment on the tenth floor of a huge building. Dad left for work early in the morning. Reshi and I began attending a school nearby, and we were both placed in the same ESL class. Mom stayed home all day. Everything around us was new and pleasant.

There were other Punjabi families in our building and also in other buildings in the area but we did not socialize with them. We didn't feel any need to. In our small world, we began to live a full life, such as we had never lived before. On Saturdays we went shopping. A couple of times we rode the subway train to go downtown. From our apartment, we could see the CN tower and were planning to go there one day. On Sundays, we went to the gurdwara. Dad's friends were priests and hymn-singers. He had told us that most of the time he had stayed with them while he was a refugee.

One day when I returned from school I saw Dad's friend Giani Manjit Singh talking to Mom. He was speaking in a very serious tone and stopped when I entered. I folded my hands and very respectfully said, Sat sri akaal. He was pleased and embraced me warmly. He spoke to me in a sweet and intimate voice and said, "Son, stay a Sikh just as you are now. Don't cut your hair like the young people here do." I liked his advice and the way he spoke to me. It made me feel proud of my dad that he had such nice friends. I put down my books and went into the kitchen to get something to eat. Giani-ji stood up to leave and I overheard him say to Mom, "With God's blessings, now that you are here, you can look after your home. A lonely man can be tempted in many ways in a strange place. What happened in the past, happened. Now you can set your family life back on track. Matters like these . . . ." He trailed off upon my return from the kitchen.

Something was not right. Having become accustomed to see Mom smiling and happy, I couldn't understand the reason for her grief, which she was trying to hide from me. After a couple of days I was awakened at night by loud voices. Mom and Dad were quarrelling. I couldn't make out anything of what they were saying but this was startling: I was unable to go back to sleep the rest of the night.

Something had shattered our peace. No matter how much I tried, I could not make any sense of what had gone wrong. In the gurdwara, I noticed people whispering among themselves and staring in our direction. Slowly it dawned on me that there was some connection between people's behaviour towards us and Mom and Dad's fight. I tried to link it to what Giani Manjit Singh had said to Mom a few days earlier, but I came up blank. Mom and Dad rarely spoke to each other. Our home was not the happy place it had been only a few days before.

Dad began to come home late from work. Mom waited impatiently for him and was always cross with us. If ever Reshi or I asked why Daddy was late, she would yell at us and end up breaking down. Life in Canada became unbearable. Reshi and I lived in fear, as we had done in Agra.

To hear anything unpleasant about my dad was painful. He showed no anger towards anyone. He was always calm. However, I could tell that like me he was troubled inside. But neither Mom nor Dad explained anything to me about the trouble that plagued our home. I didn't like being treated the same way as Reshi—like a child. I began to feel bitter towards my parents.

I remembered my days with Narinder in Agra and felt lonely at school. I was even more isolated at home, where we avoided each other as best we could.

There were three Punjabi boys always hanging around together and they jeered at me whenever they saw me. Two of the boys were really big and strong. One day after school they gathered around me and one of the bigger ones, who was wearing a turban, said, "Hey Deeshi, I hear your father's been sleeping around, eh?"

"Lucky man, screwing two women at the same time," said the

other one, making obscene gestures with his hands.

"Man, she is so nice-looking too. We see her at the gurdwara all the time," said the first one.

The third boy, who was about my size, said, "Come on you guys, leave him alone. It is not his fault."

"What is your fucking problem?" and with that they started to argue. I was scared and tried my best to control my tears. It seemed like an endless walk home that day.

I was afraid to run into them again. It was impossible to hide from them since we lived on the same street. From their taunting and other people's talk, the details of the story of my family slowly began to emerge. By the time the terrible incident took place I had mostly figured out what happened. My father, before we joined him in Toronto, lived in the gurdwara and took part in hymn-singing and readings of the Holy Granth. One day he and the other singers were invited to a young woman's home. She had been married to an older man and had become a widow. In her husband's memory she initiated an akhandpath, a continuous reading of the Holy Granth for three days. My father was one of the men taking turns reading the scriptures. An affair began between him and the widow and eventually my father moved in with her. He had no money and she needed a man around the house. Up to this point, things were plain enough. What was the reality beyond this? Why did my father kill her?

Many people were upset simply because he had hurt the image of the community and the cause of the Sikh refugees in Canada. They were not interested in the facts or details. Others enjoyed the gossip about my dad and the woman being in love with each other, the kind of love that happens in Hindi films. Another theory was that she had cast a spell on my dad such that he was unable to live without her. Some suggested that having spent so much money on him she was forcing him to leave his family for her. Who knows what the truth was? And what difference does it make now anyway? Maybe Dad really was in love with that woman. She had money and was younger and prettier than Mom.

I hated that woman as much as Mom hated Indira Gandhi. Whether Mom had no more anger left in her or she had no more desire to fight, she never showed any outrage towards that woman. Only once I heard her remark, "It was in our karma to face still another Indira in Canada." It seemed to me that she truly wanted to end the matter and was ready to compromise with Dad. She was waiting for him to do something, but what actually happened, nobody could have imagined.

It felt as if I had been murdered as well. I got sick and spent a few weeks in hospital. I asked Reshi to cut my hair the day I came home; Mom didn't say a word. Our life was more miserable than it had ever been before. Dad was in prison for murder. We didn't go anywhere and no one came to visit us. Occasionally Mom went to see Dad. One time Reshi and I accompanied her.

A week after the three of us visited Dad, two police officers came to our apartment early in the morning. Reshi and I were still in bed. Mom called me into the living room because she didn't understand what they were saying. The officers were very polite and they asked us to sit down. One sat down beside us and told us that my dad had killed himself in prison the night before.

On the advice of our family doctor, Mom decided to leave Toronto. I think it was a good decision. Ever since we came here, my health has improved and I have been working in a restaurant the last few months. I get tired from work and find it easier to fall asleep. Whenever I'm unable to sleep, I read, and sometimes I write. I have already filled more than half of this notebook.

When something unusual happens, it throws me back into depression, like today when I hit Reshi. The same thing happened two weeks ago when we received news of my grandfather's death. At such times I feel empty and worthless and I want to kill myself. I cannot escape the memory: Mom and I are running to the parking lot outside our apartment building . . . Reshi behind us, shrieking and running . . . the slowly expanding line of blood on the cement . . . Dad holding that dying woman in his arms . . . lying beside him the blood-stained axe with the flesh sticking to it . . . Mom's heart-piercing cry . . . and then blaring sirens from police cars . . . more screams . . . more deafening sounds . . .

This condition lasts a long time. Then I slowly begin to see the pain on Mom's face and the tears flowing from Reshi's eyes. I see Maan-ji's gentle face swaying above me and I feel her soft fingers touching my forehead. I hear her kind voice, "Who else will wipe your sister's tears if not you?" With this sense of belonging and responsibility, I slowly start to calm down.

Father and Son

I T WAS AROUND FIVE in the morning. There were only a few cars on the road, and in this run-down part of the city every third or fourth was a police cruiser. The area looked more dilapidated in the early morning light, and the stolid buildings stood quiet and motionless. I had already made my rounds in other parts of the city and my graveyard shift's last stop was an old department store, for which my employer, Akaal Maintenance Company, had recently acquired the janitorial contract.

I turned into the alley behind the store, and parked my car. As I passed a small building on my left, I saw an old man sitting on the back stairs. He had a loosely tied white turban on his head. Beside him lay a man covered with a long grey coat and a red baseball cap. I had never seen a turbaned Punjabi among the homeless of this area before. I went inside the store to check on the workers, but I couldn't help thinking about the old Sikh I had just seen.

After finishing my round, instead of rushing home as usual, I walked towards where I'd seen the turbaned man. It was quiet. I stepped on a rusted muffler, startling the ravens picking at a half-opened garbage bag. I held my breath against the choking stench of urine.

The man was now sitting alone. He had a long white beard that made him look very old. I greeted him, "Sat sri akaal, Baba-ji."

He looked at me in surprise. His turban was in a jumble and he seemed disoriented. I invited him for a coffee. Leaning on his cane he slowly stood up and began walking in silence. Turning right into the next street, we entered a dingy coffee shop. A thin old Chinese man sat on a stool behind the counter. There was no one else around. Baba-ji stopped briefly. He pointed me to a table, and then slowly walked towards the washroom.

I ordered two cups of coffee and some doughnuts. I'd already finished my coffee and doughnut by the time the old man got back. He looked fresh and walked in a dignified manner, having neatly re-tied his turban and combed and cleaned his long flowing beard. He cheerfully sat down across from me and briefly touched the outside of the cup with his palm to feel the warmth.

I got up and said, "Baba-ji, I'll get a hot cup for you, that one must be cold now."

He nodded and picked up one of the two doughnuts from the plate.

I returned with two fresh cups of coffee. He mixed a spoonful of sugar into his and slowly took a couple of sips. He looked at me and smiled. "What is this Baba-ji business? I may have a white beard but I am still young at heart. Some day I will show you what I mean. Even young white women are proud to sit beside me."

"I would sure like to see that," I said with a grin.

He looked at me gently, took a big gulp of coffee, and started to talk in an easy relaxed manner. "I wasn't too sure about you when I saw that bright tie around your neck so early in the morning, but you seem to be okay."

"Oh, the tie!" My hand automatically went to my neck to loosen the knot. "This is something I have to wear. You see, I am a supervisor and you know how our people are, they don't properly respect you if you don't look official."

"Yes, yes, I know." He shook his head. "To make the oxen go, you must have a strong bamboo stick in your hand. My son wears one. He also has a huge pug on his head." With his right hand, he touched his own turban. I noticed the large steel kara around his wrist that clattered each time his arm brushed the table.

Looking at it, he said, "My granddaughter-in-law brought it from Ambarsar. She is a nice, well-educated girl. Her name is Jasjit; I call her Jiti. My grandson, married to her, is an idiot. He can't even speak Punjabi properly. Jiti's parents married her to my grandson hoping to come to Canada. With love she placed this kara on my arm. I never take it off."

Trying to control his emotions he went on, "It's very useful too. You know, one day my drinking buddy Kevin picked a fight with me. We were both drunk. I just slapped him on the face, but the kara slashed away part of his ear. I felt bad and I looked after him for a whole week. But everyone else is afraid of me now. 'Watch for Singh's weapon,' they say."

Baba finished the coffee, stared at the empty plate, and said, "Son, get me a couple more of these doughnuts."

I brought back two more doughnuts and a fresh cup of coffee. "Baba," I said, "you were going to tell me about your white girl friends."

"I'll tell you all that in time." Holding the doughnut up in his hand he said, "Why do they cut out the middle of these dough-nuts like the old British coins in India?"

"Baba, you know these whites are very stylish people, they even like to make special designs on food."

"Yeah! This is a good design, a real reflection of today's world—whatever substance there is, it's all outside. There's nothing in the centre—just emptiness."

After a short pause he continued in his philosophical mood, "These big lovers of design sure take a large chunk of the doughnut away. It seems to me that they always have some hidden motive behind their designs."

"Were you involved with the communists in your younger days, Baba?"

He smiled. "Everybody who comes from Punjab has heard communists talk." After a pause and looking straight into my eyes he said, "But I can't quite figure you out."

"What is it that you don't understand about me?"

"Those who wear bright ties like you and especially those who supervise other people, usually don't have time for someone like me. And here you are, not only talking to me but also buying me coffee and doughnuts. How come you are in such a rotten business?"

"You have to work to make a living in this country, Baba. And you don't always get to choose what you do."

"Still, if you don't like what you do, it can make you miserable in the long run."

"Never mind about me. Let's talk about your girl friends."

"What is there to talk about? The poor souls—they just try to exist as well as they can."

Just then, Baba saw one of his friends enter the coffee shop. He waved him over. "Harvey, come, coffee." An aged, sickly man walked slowly towards our table.

I brought another three doughnuts and two cups of coffee. In his broken English, Baba was telling Harvey, "Nice boy, he supervasor, you know."

Harvey made no secret of the fact the he was only interested in food, and paid not the slightest attention to me.

"Harvey, me, good friends," Baba told me happily and watched Harvey go at the doughnuts.

"Like you, Harvey is a family man and used to work in a big office. But he got tired of the rat race and left everything behind. He is a very decent fellow, hardly ever talks. He's friends with Kevin too, the guy I cut with my kara. Kevin is from a reserve up north near the Prince Rupert area and used to work with some Punjabis in a sawmill. My friends are the best people around here. I only know just a little bit of English. It makes no difference to them. When we're drunk, I speak Punjabi and they tell me their stories in English. If somebody tries to harass me or something, they're always ready to defend me. When we receive our welfare cheques we rent a hotel room together."

"Where do you manage to stay the rest of the time?"

"What is there to manage? We sleep where we happen to be after drinking beer."

"And where do you get the money for drinking?"

"Oh, we stand around here and there and ask for some loose change. We say, 'You have change? We need change for bus to go home'. When we have enough for a round of beer, we go into the beer parlour."

He quickly added, "No, no, I don't beg. I know begging is the most disgraceful thing to do for a Punjabi. Harvey and Kevin ask for change. I only stand around with them. Anyway, we don't behave like the beggars in India. If somebody gives us some change, fine, if not, we don't harass them or anything."

"What do you do for food and all the rest?"

"When we have money, we eat in a restaurant, and when we don't, we eat in the soup kitchen."

Harvey was busy with his coffee and doughnuts. I wasn't too sure whether he disliked me or whether he was not interested because we were talking in Punjabi. He didn't look at me or say thank you. After he finished his coffee he got up and said to Baba, "Boor, let's go and sit in the park, it's nice and sunny outside."

"Yeah, nice day! You go, me come later."

Baba gave me an explanation for his name. "They don't know how to say our hard 'r' sound. My name is Boor Singh but they just call me Boor."

He watched Harvey walk slowly out the door and then asked me, "Where do you live, son?"

"In Surrey."

"Would you do me another favour today? On your way home, could you drop me near the big gurdwara? I haven't seen Jiti's little daughter for many days. Now, talking to you today, I feel like going home."

We left the coffee shop and walked over to my car. As soon as we had cleared the first traffic light, I called home to check if the kids were getting ready for school. Nobody picked up the phone. The company had recently given me a cell phone and I loved to use it every chance I got.

Baba was shaking his head. "What will become of people like you? You are a slave to these little shrieking boxes twenty-four hours a day. Do you ever think about life?"

The scolding made me thoughtful for a few moments. Perhaps to break the silence that followed, or perhaps because he felt guilty about chastizing me, he said, "Son, you are not the only one, everybody seems to be doing the same thing. My son also has these boxes and whatnot tied to his waist."

"What does your son do?"

"He does his mother's . . . " He didn't complete the curse. But he sounded extremely upset.

He finally said, "He sells insurance or something."

"He must have a good business."

"Oh sure, he's very successful in his business. He is a leader in the community too. You know, the kind we have parading around in every corner of our community nowadays?"

He paused to look at me and then continued, "Ever since my son became interested in this leadership business, he has lost touch with his soul. When he began to tie his turban again after so many years, I was very happy. The turban completely transforms a person. You are almost like royalty, different from everyone around you. But my son not only changed his looks, he completely changed as a person."

"What happened?"

"He came to Canada when he was still young. For years he lived with his uncle and didn't communicate with us much. When he got married, he needed his mother to look after the children. First came his mother, then I followed. She babysat his kids for many years. Couple of years ago she had a heart attack and died."

The road ahead was blocked by an accident and we almost came to a stop. Baba continued his story, paying no attention to how slow we were moving or the chaos around us.

"I have been here for more than ten years now. In the beginning, we got along well at home. We ate well, drank regularly, and had good times with the kids. I went to India after my wife died and stayed in the village for a few months. I was lonely in the large house. So I returned. Life became a bearable routine. But then my son became involved in gurdwara politics. It happened right after Indira Gandhi attacked the Golden Temple.

You know the whole Sikh community was upset. That's when everything changed. A lot of simple people turned fanatics overnight. My son also became a puritan and began issuing orders not to bring any meat or liquor in the house."

Baba pulled out a wrinkled napkin from his jacket and wiped his face, which was nearly hidden by his white beard. With a sharp, painful look in his eyes, he began his story again.

"There was no room for me in the house, unless I quit drinking. I went to live and work on a farm in Abbotsford for a few months. I didn't like it there. In the village, I had spent my whole life working in my own fields and had other people working for me. At this age to work for some greedy Punjabi farmer was the most terrible thing.

"Then I figured, why do I have to work so hard anyway. What do I need the money for? I didn't have a handful of daughters that I had to get married off. So why should I go and work in the farms, dragging myself along strawberry rows like a dog with a broken lower back? I was able to get welfare with the help of a social worker. Now I stay with my friends and do what I want. I have no worry in the world. I don't go to my son's home often; sometimes, when I feel like seeing the children, I go during the day when my son isn't home."

"Hasn't your son tried to bring you back to the house?"

"The last time I went to see Jiti's little daughter he happened to be home with a friend. He said, 'Bhaiaa, your behaviour is ruining my reputation in the community. You should act your age, stay home and put your mind to worshipping God as you are supposed to in your old age.'

"I said, 'Son, I'm not against worshipping God, but I don't feel the need to do it, and I don't want to do it.'

"You know what he said to me? He said, 'Then get rid of this turban and hair from your head and shave your beard.'

"That made me angry! I said, 'You have no right to tell me what to do. I have lived like this all my life, I am not going to cut my hair and take the turban off just because you say so.'

"His friend Kirpal Singh also joined in. 'Uncle-ji, when you stand on Hastings Street with your turban and beard and beg for money, we feel that is an insult to the whole Sikh community. These are crucial times for our community. We are persecuted everywhere. We have to be extra careful to protect our image.'

"I said to him, 'I don't particularly want to do that, it is your friend here who doesn't allow me to stay in the house. So I go and live with my friends.'

"My son said to Kirpal Singh, 'I don't stop him from drinking. I only ask him to do it discreetly.'

"Kirpal Singh added, 'Yes, Uncle-ji, everybody does these kinds of things behind closed doors. You should realize that your son, Mr Jagmohan Singh, has a big reputation in the community.'

"It was becoming hard for me to sit there. I said, 'Kirpal, you are a sensible man, but what you are asking me to do is wrong. I have never done anything in secret in my life and I am not about to start now.'

"Kirpal Singh said, 'We are not asking you to deceive any body. Now you look at us, your son and I, we often go to business meetings and parties. When colleagues offer us wine or beer, we don't refuse it. In such company, you have to act like the rest of the people, otherwise you can't be successful. But when we go to gatherings of our own people, we humbly refuse it. We tell them we don't touch this stuff; it is against the teachings of our Sikh Gurus. That is how things are done here and that is what we are asking you to do, nothing more, and nothing out of the ordinary. Do whatever you want to, but in the secrecy of your own home, not in public, that's all.'

"And my son said, 'We are really concerned about your safety, because we think that the people you stay with are dangerous. Everybody is afraid of them. The newspapers are full of stories about drug dealers and drunks killing each other with knives and guns in those beer parlours.'

"I was annoyed. I said, 'Who is going to steal anything from me? Why would someone kill me for no reason? I have friends who would die for me; maybe you are afraid, I'm not.'

"That was three months ago. I have not gone back since."

Baba looked at the streets more carefully now and knew that we were near his son's house. Finishing the story, he said, "That is the situation with my son, Sardar Jagmohan Singh, the big community leader. But I can't stay away from Jiti and her little daughter for too long, so I visit them once in a while."

He pointed towards a street coming up ahead and said, "Drop me at the corner, Son. It was so good talking in our own language with you today."

I stopped the car at the intersection and waited for Baba-ji to step out. He opened the door, putting his cane out on the pavement first. As he lifted his right foot to get out, his eyes darted towards his son's house. He stopped for a few seconds, and then pulled his cane back in, closing the door behind him. He mumbled something I didn't quite hear.

Then he said, "My son's car is there; he must be home for lunch or something. I will come back some other day to see the child. Drop me at the bus stop on Fraser Street."

He sat quietly in the car. At the bus stop he stepped out, turned towards me, and said in a very warm but tired voice, "Have a happy and prosperous life, Beta."

He slowly started to walk towards the bench at the bus stop, to sit there unsheltered, all alone, by the sidewalk.

Eyes in the Dark

HIS WIFE KULVIR AND HIS new-born daughter were both sleeping, and the nurse told Parminder that they would probably sleep through the night. He decided to leave, but it was early Friday evening and he didn't want to go home. He stopped in the hospital lobby and called his friend Piara to invite him over for a few drinks. Piara, who lived alone in a two-bedroom apartment in an old three-storey building in East Vancouver, insisted that he should come over to his house instead.

When Parminder entered Piara's living room he was surprised to see the place comparatively clean and Piara all dressed up as if ready to go some place. After shaking hands with Parminder, Piara immediately picked up the bottle of scotch that sat on the kitchen table, poured the liquor into two glasses, and said, "Do you want water or something else with your drink?"

"Water," Parminder said. Again, he was surprised at Piara's quickness.

"Man, I got worried about you ever since you told me this morning that your wife had a baby girl. I know how it is. I thought you probably needed cheering up." Piara emptied his glass and placed it back on the table.

"Oh, I'm okay," Parminder said.

"Have you called your folks back home?" asked Piara.

"No, not yet. I don't know how to tell them. I know my parents were really hoping for a grandson." Parminder pulled a chair away from the kitchen table to sit and said, "How are things with you?"

"Things couldn't be better. I've been on compensation for the last few weeks, nothing to do, life is good."

"What's the matter? You seem to be a bit nervous about something."

"Oh, nothing, yaar. You know my friend Nanju; I think you met him here once. He was supposed to come an hour ago. I don't know if the bastard is going to show up or not."

Piara went to the living room window to look. On his way back he poured another drink, sat across from Parminder, and said, "You know, some people have all the luck in the world. Nanju has found this native Indian woman. She is from Prince Rupert or somewhere near there. She looks just like a Punjabi woman and even understands and speaks a bit of Punjabi. She can cook our food, does all the work in the house. I heard that she was married to a Punjabi and when he got his immigration status, he kicked her out. She has a three- or four-year-old son and that bastard didn't care about the boy either."

Parminder listened silently. Sara came to his mind, but then there were so many other Punjabis who had married native Indian women in order to get landed status.

Piara went to the window again. He saw Nanju's car stop in front of his house. He jumped with pleasure. "He is here and she is with him. Maybe it's my lucky night too."

Nanju walked in, supporting a drunk woman, followed by a scared little boy who was holding a teddy bear under his arm. Nanju sat the woman on the sofa and said to Piara, "Brother! She had too much to drink and didn't want to come."

Nanju shook hands with both Piara and Parminder. Piara gave the boy a cookie and asked him if he wanted to watch TV. The boy nodded. Piara took him into the next room where he had a small TV. The boy passed by Parminder and looked at him in the same expressionless way he had looked at Piara. For a moment, Parminder thought he had seen those eyes before.

He turned towards the woman to look at her but she had slid sideways on the sofa and her face was hidden behind her arm.

Nanju had gone to the bathroom and Piara was still in the other room with the boy. Parminder got up from the chair, poured a big drink of scotch, and gulped it down. He could not bring himself to look in the direction of the sofa again. He picked up his jacket and left.

He sat in the car for a few minutes before starting it. He did not want to admit that the woman he had just seen was Sara; those expressionless eyes of the little boy haunted him. He thought of going back to the hospital, it was only eight o'clock. He fondly recalled Kulvir's face, so clear and tender after giving birth, but when he tried to imagine his new-born daughter, he could only see the rounded face of the little boy with a cookie in his hand, staring at him as he walked behind Piara.

Parminder drove aimlessly for a while and then parked his car by John Hendry Park. He walked to Trout Lake in the middle of the park. There weren't many trees by the water and there was just enough light to see his way. He stood staring in the dark, recalling how he had walked around this little lake with Sara and sat on these benches by the water with her hundreds of times.

Sara came to live next door to the house where he had moved
in upon arriving from India. He lived with the Johals, from
Nangal, his own village back in Punjab. It was a small house,
and they lived on the main floor while renting out the basement. Parminder shared a room with Balbir, the youngest of
three brothers. The eldest, Charan, worked in a sawmill and
Harbans worked in a meat-packing plant. Both Charan and
Harbans were married, but their wives were still in India. To
cover Parminder's expenses, his father had made arrangements
with their family back in Nangal.

Soon after arriving as a visitor in 1973, Parminder applied
to become a permanent resident of Canada. He had to hire a
lawyer because the immigration department had become sus-
picious of the large number of Punjabi visitors applying for
landed status. His lawyer was able to get him extensions to stay
longer in Canada, but permanent status was still out of reach.

Many of their friends who came over to visit the four men
were also single. Their talk often involved their longing for
women. Occasionally, Charan and his friends went to a beer
parlour in Vancouver's skid-row area in search of women.
Sometimes a friend of Harbans brought a middle-aged native
woman to the house. Parminder quickly learned that native
women were more accepting of Punjabi men than white women
were. He had learned English in school and could understand it
fairly well, but found it hard to speak. However, talking to these
women, who were often drunk, helped him gain confidence
speaking English.

It was on a sunny day in early December that he first noticed a
girl next door. As he found out later that evening from Charan,
she was Gordon's niece. Gordon worked with Charan in a
sawmill in South Vancouver and they often shared a ride. Her

name was Sara and she was twenty years old, a year younger than Parminder.

Sara's hair and eyes were black and she looked Punjabi. Parminder watched her and wanted to talk to her but was hesitant. He noticed one day that she was also watching him. She was sitting on the front porch and Parminder, standing by the fence outside his house, said hello. He introduced himself as Peter, explaining to Sara that it was short for a long and hard name. They went to see a movie the next evening.

Harbans, who had seen Parminder talking to Sara, later said to him, "Hey Peter, don't forget to share with others, it's not right to eat the whole dish all by yourself, you know. You can always get another one easily because you know English. I don't speak the language so I can only take what others leave for me."

Parminder laughed. Charan, who was also sitting there, said, "Parminder, if you have any sense get this Indian girl to marry you."

"Just watch me, brother, that is exactly what I am working on," Parminder said slyly.

Sara had spent most of her life in a small remote reserve up north. She had only come to Vancouver a few times for short visits. She didn't have any friends here in the big city. In her innocent way, she told Parminder to stop when he tried to kiss her while they were walking in the park. "Why not, Sara, there is no one here who knows us," said Parminder grabbing her by her arms.

"I am afraid to fall in love with anyone. I know people get hurt," Sara said. She went and sat on a bench by the pond.

Parminder followed her. He gently held her hand and said, "Sara, I am a good person. You can trust me."

"Peter, I am not saying you are bad; it's just that something happened to my sister."

"What happened to your sister?"

Sara looked at Parminder for a brief moment and then started to tell her sister's story as if she were telling it to herself. "Janet was five years older than me. She was much more prettier than I am—she was so nice too—and she knew everything—how to talk to boys and all. She loved me a lot. Then Robert, a white boy from Edmonton, came to our reserve with my cousin Steve. My sister fell in love with him and went away to Edmonton. She hugged me before she left—I cried—she cried too. She told me to look after our dad and she said she would write. She never did. She came back a year and a half later with a one-month-old baby—Robert had left her. After a while she went away again and we don't know where she is now."

Sara was crying.

Parminder held her close to him and said in a soft voice, "Nobody will ever leave you Sara, I love you." Sara responded by holding him tightly in her arms.

Parminder went home and told Charan, "Well, brother, I have done my part. Now go and talk to her uncle so that we can arrange something quickly before I have to go and get another extension from Immigration."

Parminder married Sara in a courtroom in the beginning of April. As soon as he received his social insurance number, Harbans found him a job in the meat-packing plant where he worked.

Parminder and Sara moved into a small basement apartment. While staying with the Johals he had learned to make roti and cook Punjabi dals and vegetables. The three brothers often praised him for his tasty curry chicken. He taught Sara some Punjabi dishes to cook. In many ways, she was like a typical Punjabi girl. She did not drink or smoke and never went outside the house by herself. She kept the little place clean, cooked for Parminder, washed his clothes, and more than anything else, she loved him. After a while, Parminder started to offer her liquor, which she refused at first, but then began to have a drink or two with him, especially on weekends.

Six months after they moved into their own place, Sara's father became seriously ill, and she went to see him and ended up staying two months. Parminder spoke to her on the phone a few times but didn't insist too much on her coming back.

She arrived on a bus one Saturday afternoon. Parminder took her to a restaurant to eat in the evening. Later at home, he offered her a drink. She was very happy to be back and gladly took the drink. Parminder poured her more drinks until she was quite drunk.

Parminder, acting drunk, asked her, "Sara, were you drinking while you were away?"

"No, Peter, I never touched the damn thing." Drunk as she was, Sara gazed at Parminder, her hurt showing in her eyes. She tried to embrace Parminder. "I love you, Peter, I wouldn't even think of drinking with anyone else."

"Don't give me that bullshit. You are no different than the rest of the Indian whores. I know that you have been drinking and sleeping around all this time. No wonder you didn't want to come back to Vancouver."

Sara angrily picked up her half-full glass of liquor and threw it at Parminder. He ducked, and then started to beat her. He was careful not to hit her in a way that would draw blood or show. Parminder had behaved in a calculated manner, just as he had planned for weeks. Sara didn't want to stay with him. She called a cab and went to her cousins in North Vancouver. She returned to her father the next day.

Sara and her father came to stay with her uncle the following winter. Parminder managed to convince Sara to come and live with him again. She was a changed person now. She sat quietly most of the time, looking sad and disoriented. She drank beer, wine, hard liquor, whatever she was offered. This was exactly what Parminder was hoping for. He was a landed immigrant now and wanted to legally divorce Sara so he could go back to Punjab to get married there. His lawyer had prepared all the necessary papers for him. It was easy to get Sara drunk and to sign the divorce papers. Sara in her innocent way told him that she had missed her period and she might be pregnant with his baby. She had been with him more than six weeks, and he wanted her out immediately. He got her drunk again and accused her of sleeping around like before. This time he put her on the Prince Rupert bus himself.

Parminder found work in a sawmill in New Westminster that paid better than the meat-packing job, and moved close to his new place of work. He stopped seeing his old friends, and the Johals. Sara would not have found him even if she had tried to.

Parminder lived alone, drove a cab on weekends, and bought a house in New Westminster within a year. He kept a portion of the basement for himself and rented the rest of the house to a large white family. The rent more than covered the mortgage.

Three months after he bought the house, he went back to India. He married Kulvir, a girl selected by his parents. She was a first-year student in a master's program at Punjab State University, Chandigarh. She abandoned her studies and came to Canada with him. Parminder had a new life. He socialized with only a few friends, and a few families related to Kulvir. Piara was one of his new friends.

He sat on a bench by the lake that used to be Sara's favourite place. He didn't resist anymore the thought of who the woman had been in Piara's apartment. He sat looking into the dark water and saw clearly the expressionless eyes of his son watching him.

The Song

CHARAN SINGH RAISED HIS HEAD to look at the clock as he had done many times during the night. It was only three in the morning.

He was angry at the silver clock, sitting on the small table by his bed. The alarm was permanently set at 6:00 AM but he was always up before it rang. Yesterday morning, however, he was still asleep when the alarm rang and it woke up the tenants in the next room. The white couple that rented the basement suite started kicking the walls and later complained to his son Jaswant, who blamed him, "You just don't know how to live among white people."

Charan Singh had got along fine with the lady who rented the basement before this couple moved in. She was a bit on the heavy side, Charan Singh had thought, when he saw her for the first time, but the approving big smile on her face made him lose all fear he had of white people. She would try to talk to him even though he knew only a few words of English. Her name was Joyce. He had difficulty saying it and called her "Joce." At first she tried to correct him but then she would simply laugh. Charan Singh also found it funny the way she said his name, "Sharaan." Many times Joyce had knocked on his door to share coffee with him, and he could recall its fresh aroma. It seemed to Charan Singh that she well understood his situation and was always sympathetic. Joyce's eighteen-year-old daughter lived with her and she, too, was polite and friendly.

Joyce was a little late in paying the rent a couple of times, and his son used this as an excuse to throw her out. Charan Singh told his friend Jawala Singh, "My son has become so greedy that it doesn't make sense any more. He kicked that nice lady Joce out just for a bit of more money. This new couple drinks every night till two in the morning, plays loud music, and they don't get up till the middle of the day."

After the scolding from his son, and out of fear that it might again disturb the tenants, he didn't set his alarm last night. Worried, he was unable to sleep till midnight and now he was up again. There was complete silence in the basement, but no peace in his mind. Not that he had never been scolded by his son before, but for some reason he was more hurt this time. He thought about his wife Balwant Kaur who was now living with their younger daughter in Calgary. He missed her more at times like these. He wanted to tell her how they had moved his bed to this tiny room in the basement when Surjit's sister and brother-in-law came to live with them. He had been more than a year now in this cold and isolated room. At the time Jaswant had said, "It'll probably take a month or so before they find a place to live, and then we will move your bed back to your room on the main floor."

He remembered his old home, built outside the village on a small ten-acre family farm. He never had any problem falling asleep in the fresh open air in the midst of growing crops. Just before he fell asleep each night, he would lie gazing at the clear night sky and regarded those familiar stars as part of his being, the same way he felt about his fields and his animals. Here now, in this tiny room, all he saw or imagined in the dark was a light bulb hanging in the middle of the low ceiling. Once he had not been careful and received a sharp look from his daughter-in-law for breaking the bulb.

He considered getting up and turning the light on but gave up the idea and tried to get some more sleep. He closed his eyes and pressed the old rajai under his legs and hips, but the cold penetrated his bones. It had been snowing the last two days and the nights were bitterly cold. There was no heat in the room. The glass window, covered by a thick gray cloth, didn't open. He had placed a small mat by his bed to avoid the dreadful touch of the cold cement floor.

In a few hours it would be time to go to work. The thought of work made him even angrier. Delivering advertising flyers to people's homes all over the city was not an easy job, especially when it snowed.

Unable to get back to sleep, he could do nothing but lie there and again ponder the question: What happened to their dream of a good and happy life here in Canada?

Charan Singh and Balwant Kaur came to Canada in 1973 to help their son Jaswant raise his family. A lot had happened in the fourteen years since then.

When they came, they were disappointed to see that their son and his family were living in a rented basement apartment while all their relatives and village folks owned their own homes. But for years Jaswant had regularly sent money to them in India so that his two sisters could be married. He had a steady job in a sawmill, but his wife Surjit Kaur didn't work in order to look after their young children, a three-year-old boy and two-year-old girl.

Charan Singh said to his wife, "We should help Jaswant buy his own home and live like everyone else." Balwant Kaur agreed. "Yes, our son helped us for years. Our younger daughter will come to Canada with her in-laws by next year and by the will of God the older one will also make it to Canada one day. We don't have to worry about them any more."

"I should find some work," Charan Singh said, in a bid to put the burden on himself.

Balwant Kaur replied, "I have already told Surjit Kaur that I'll look after the kids now and she should find a job somewhere."

"So what did she say?"

"She said, Bibi-ji, you both have just come from India, I want to serve you and make you happy."

Charan Singh was pleased. "Our son has always been good and now his wife is even more respectful. Remember how worried we used to get back in the village, when we heard horrible stories of how some daughters-in-law mistreated their in-laws in Canada?"

"We must have done some good deeds in our past lives, and now we are reaping the benefits. It is all a khel of kismet, the game of luck."

Jaswant at first didn't want his wife to work outside the home, but eventually he agreed, and she was able to find a job as a seamstress in a clothing factory. Charan Singh started to go to the farms with Hazara Singh, who was from the same village and lived close by. Early in the morning they travelled in a farm contractor's crowded van to the Chilliwack area. It was a long tiresome drive to and from the farms and it would be dark in the evening when they returned. Charan Singh didn't care how

74

hard the work was, he was happy that he was earning to help his son, and at the same time he was among people who spoke his own language. Initially he only knew Hazara Singh, but soon he was friendly with many other men who were from his own area in the Punjab.

In the evenings the entire family ate together sitting around the small table in a room that was their kitchen, sitting room and family room combined. Balwant Kaur would try to stop the kids from running and making noise and would mockingly complain, "This is how they make me run after them all day! They just don't listen to me at all!"

Charan Singh teased her, "Well, it is up to you, if you don't want to stay here, in a warm room with a nice carpet, then you can go to the farms and enjoy the back-breaking work all day! I'll look after these little trouble-makers myself!"

Balwant Kaur laughed. "Na, Baba, that is your job, why should I go to the farms? My son is earning, my daughter-in-law is earning, and you are earning, what more can *I* do?"

Jaswant would join in, "Bibi, if you really want to go to the farms, then we can find someone to look after the kids."

And Surjit would come to her mother-in-law's defense. "You keep your schemes to yourself, we are not going to send our Bey-ji to the farms, no matter what happens."

Enjoying their teasing, Balwant Kaur would call her little grandson, who kept everybody amused with his baby talk, "Veh Deepia, look, your father is going to send me to the farms with your grandfather, should I go with him? Will you look after your little sister Rani all by yourself?"

Deepa would come running from whatever he was doing and put his arms around his grandmother's neck and yell out: "No, no, you're not going to the farms!" They would all laugh at his quick reaction.

Within a year, they bought their house. They had the akhand-path performed right after they moved and invited all their relatives and friends. Everyone congratulated Charan Singh and Balwant Kaur, not only for their new home, but also for being so lucky in their son and daughter-in-law's behaviour. The basement of their newly bought home was not yet finished, and many guests gave their opinion as to how it could best be developed to get the maximum rent from it. Make two separate suites, they suggested, rent one out and keep one for yourself. Charan Singh thought that was a sensible thing to do, but Jaswant surprised everyone by saying that he was not going to rent his basement out. His mortgage was not more than the rent he had been paying before buying the home, so he was used to making monthly payments.

Charan Singh was filled with pride for his son. Hazara Singh said, "There aren't many sons like your Jaswant in Canada nowadays, I can tell you that. The very air of this land is poisoned with money; nobody is able to see beyond it. This is the first time I have heard someone say that he is not going to rent his basement out. Bravo, all the more power to your son, Charan Singh. I wish everybody had a son like your Jaswant."

In the basement, Jaswant made a cozy rec room for the children to play and a bar for entertaining friends. Charan Singh continued to work on the farms and during the off season he drew unemployment insurance benefits. Surjit held on to her sewing job, and the family lived comfortably. Two years after they bought the house, both Charan Singh and Balwant Kaur went to India at Jaswant's insistence. They had the best time of their lives during that trip. They gave money to the poor and donated to many sacred places including Baba Tana, their ancestral village. Everyone in the village was talking about the good fortune of their family, and especially how noble a son

Jaswant had turned out.

Three months after their return from India, a couple of events changed their lives forever. The sewing factory where Surjit worked closed down, and she was unable to find another job because she became pregnant. They had to make a suite in the basement to rent out to help with the mortgage payments. Then Jaswant had a car accident, which to Charan Singh was the cause of the end of their happiness.

Jaswant sustained minor injuries in the accident but showed no signs of going back to work. Charan Singh asked Jaswant, "Son, it seems that you have fully recovered from your injuries, how come you are not returning to work?"

"I'm getting paid while sitting at home, why should I work?"

"Still, one should be honest; if you feel okay, you should go back." Charan Singh was afraid that Jaswant would lose his job.

"Bhaya, father, I'm not cheating or doing anything wrong. Workers can collect wages while sick or injured, and that is what I'm doing."

Both Charan Singh and Balwant Kaur were worried, but Jaswant told them that he was fighting a court case with the insurance company. He did return to work and after a few months won his case and received a large sum of money. Balwant Kaur thanked God for their son's victory. They made plans to take the whole family to India.

But that trip never happened. With the money Jaswant bought some land to build a house. Charan Singh didn't see the need for another house, and he especially disliked the idea that they would have to borrow money from the bank. He saw no wisdom in the decision, but changed his mind when Jaswant explained his plan to him. "We will build the house and then sell it. We'll easily make forty to fifty thousand dollars profit from it." Charan Singh was delighted.

Jaswant worked full time at his job at the sawmill and started building the house on the side. Charan Singh was fascinated by the process; as he explained to his wife, "You hire one contractor to build the frame, another to put up the roof, yet another to install electricity in the house and so on. It's just that easy, nothing to it."

However, as they were to find out slowly and painfully, things were not that simple. Jaswant was busy every day after work and on weekends as well—having the plans drawn and passed by the city, making deals with contractors—always rushing from one thing to the other. He had no time to talk to anyone, even the children. When he was on night shift, he got only a few hours of sleep. Most of the contractors were Punjabis, offering cheaper rates, but they either failed to finish the work on time or created new problems.

Charan Singh spent most of his time in chores related to the building project. Jaswant would ask him to move the dirt from one side to the other, or pile unused lumber to the side of the house, or something. If there was no work to be done then Jaswant would tell him to keep watch on a contractor and his crew.

Charan Singh had always worked hard but had never felt this strange kind of pressure in his life before. Tired and perturbed, he would complain to Balwant Kaur, "What kind of life is this, that a person feels like he is hanging by the neck all day. Ever since the boy started this business of building house, he has neither taken a moment's break himself nor allowed anybody else to relax even for a minute."

Balwant Kaur also felt the same way. "Jaswant is always in an angry mood. Yesterday when I asked him to take Rani to see a doctor, he shouted at me."

There was a great sense of relief and jubilation when the house was finished and sold even before the carpet was laid.

Jaswant told his parents that he had made a net profit of over fifty thousand dollars. Balwant Kaur was the happiest at the prospect of taking a trip to India with the family. But they were shocked when Jaswant bought two more lots to build houses on. Charan Singh pleaded with Jaswant. "This business is not as easy as we first thought. All day you work on your job at the mill and then you have to look after the family as well. In the last few months you have had no time at all for the kids."

"There are always problems when you do something for the first time; you'll see how smoothly things move now," answered Jaswant in a decisive tone.

Charan Singh knew there was no use trying to stop him, but he tried again anyway. "Son, money is important, but it should not become more important than family."

Jaswant got angry. "You have no idea what you are talking about! Who do you think I'm doing this for, if not for the family? The real estate market is hot, this is the perfect time to make money, then we can have it easy for the rest of our lives."

Jaswant and Surjit made all the important decisions without consulting the parents. During the summer months Charan Singh worked on the farms and on weekends he helped Jaswant in his construction business. Jaswant was constantly looking for empty lots to build new houses. He had made a considerable amount of money.

Charan Singh and Balwant Kaur didn't dare to interfere, but they saw things changing for the worse. The kids stopped speaking Punjabi at home. Like their parents, they were disrespectful to the grandparents. Jaswant had no time for family matters, which worried his father and mother.

To keep his Punjabi contractors and workers happy, Jaswant would offer them drinks after work. Charan Singh saw that Jaswant himself was becoming a regular drinker. He now owned a number of lots and a few older homes that he was renting out, and at any given time he was building one or two houses. He still kept his sawmill job but regularly took days off work.

Charan Singh would hear from others about the growing business and wealth of his son and how he was friends with the politicians and the powerful people of the gurdwara. He was not sure if he should be happy when he heard such praises for his son. Balwant Kaur was still holding on to the idea of going to India and she begged Jaswant, "Son, when you had your accident I had pledged to hold a religious ceremony in our village. Please let me keep my pledge." He replied that there were all kinds of problems in Punjab for the Sikhs.

However, to please his mother, he promised, "We will have an akhandpath here and I will send some money for a religious ceremony in India. And when the situation improves in Punjab we will all go there for a visit."

Balwant Kaur didn't really believe him as far as the trip to India was concerned, but she was pleased with his readiness to have the akhandpath in Vancouver. And true to his word, Jaswant did have the akhandpath in the large local gurdwara. In fact, to Charan Singh's surprise, Jaswant started to hold the akhandpath every year. But this was, as Charan Singh soon realized, only a respectable excuse to invite his building contractors and acquaintances for a meal and drinks. Since he donated large sums to the gurdwara, he was consulted by both competing parties at the time of the gurdwara elections each year. Jaswant, to Charan Singh's dismay, had worked out a scheme with the administrators of the gurdwara. Of the money he spent on akhandpaths, he received most of it back through income tax exemptions. It seemed that in his greed Jaswant was trying to deceive even God.

Balwant Kaur found it hard to accept the idea of not being

able to take the family to India. The day she left for Calgary, she cried and said to Charan Singh, "I had great hope and excitement at the thought of taking Deepa, Rani, and Raji to our village. I wanted to do so many things there with the kids."

"No one can be happy without the blessings of Waheguru. Now our son has no dearth of money, but he has no soul left anymore," Charan Singh said.

"What is left of the family now?" sighed Balwant Kaur.

Charan Singh knew that she was also thinking about what had happened to Deepa a few weeks before. They had hardly talked about it, but it was on their minds the whole time. Deepa was getting into trouble at school and was suspended for weeks at a time. Then he was caught stealing from a store. A few days later a policeman came to their house and handcuffed Deepa and took him away while both Charan Singh and Balwant Kaur watched with shock. Charan Singh had never experienced anything like that himself, though he had seen other people from his village being arrested by police. It was the most disgraceful thing that could happen to a person.

Balwant Kaur tried to philosophize over the situation, saying, "Sweetness comes only from the amount of gur you put in the karah. Jaswant has no time for his family. How can we blame Deepa for what he does? He is young and has no sense."

"One could die in shame," said Charan Singh angrily. "I felt like hitting my head against the wall the day the policeman took Deepa in handcuffs in front of our own eyes. It is not an easy thing to accept. But what can we do? And look at the mother and father—it seems to make no difference to them. As if nothing has happened! For God's sake, such a terrible thing has befallen the family! The boy has committed a theft and was caught, they should feel some shame!"

Deepa was back home the next day. He was allowed to take

his car and stay out late as he had always done since receiving a new sports car for his sixteenth birthday a year ago. A couple of times Charan Singh tried to talk to Deepa, who only responded in an insulting manner.

"Only God can save this family now," sighed Balwant Kaur, wiping tears from her eyes.

"For how long do they want you in Calgary?" asked Charan Singh.

"Who knows?"

"I wish I could go with you. I find it so hard to live here."

"Calgary is no better. Besides, you can't come and live in your daughter's home—what would people say?"

"I guess you are right. But did they say anything at all about how long you will stay there?" Charan Singh asked again.

"It depends on our son and his wife, when and how I come back. Calgary is not like Phagwara, from where I can simply hop on a tonga and come home to my village whenever I feel like," Balwant Kaur said, irritated. He turned and looked at her in surprise.

How much she had changed, he thought sadly. He himself was not the same person anymore. There had been peace and calmness in his heart even through difficult times, but now he was always angry. He was unable to stop working as hard as he could, as if he was being pushed.

He looked at the clock, it was close to five now. He lifted the curtain and looked outside through the small window. It was snowing. "You too can do your best to hurt me," he murmured, chiding the snow or whoever was responsible for it. Suddenly he remembered the contractor Karam Singh telling him about delivering flyers in the Richmond area today. In many parts of Richmond there were no concrete sidewalks, which made it difficult to walk in the snow.

His friend Jawala Singh had told him the very first winter he worked as a flyer deliverer, "Charan Singh, if you ever decide to work in the snow, make sure you have an extra pair of heavy socks with you, but the best thing is to stay away from work when it snows." He admired Jawala Singh, a sixty-year-old, big-shouldered, fearless man, for his clear thinking. They had worked together at delivering papers now for more than three months. He shared with him everything about his son and daughter-in-law. One evening they finished their work late and he stayed overnight at Jawala Singh's.

Jawala Singh shared the basement suite with another fellow Punjabi. It had two bedrooms, one small living room, a kitchen, and a bathroom. Sitting on the kitchen chairs they took off their work shoes. Charan Singh asked, "Where is your partner today?"

"He only comes home when he feels like it, especially on days when he has received his welfare check."

"Doesn't he have a family or somebody?" asked Charan Singh casually.

Jawala Singh stared at him for a moment. Throwing his socks carelessly, he said, "You and I have families Charan Singh, what difference does it make in this country, whether you have a family or not, now tell me? Nobody is able to see beyond their own bellies here."

Jawala Singh got up from his chair and said to Charan Singh, "You go ahead and take a shower first. I'll make some tea for us. Then we'll make some roti a little later."

Charan Singh obeyed him like a child and went into the bathroom. When he came out he heard the melodious sound of algoze, a pair of traditional Punjabi flutes played together, coming from the tape recorder in the kitchen. The old familiar music gave Charan Singh a strange feeling of joy such as he hadn't felt for a long time. Jawala Singh was standing next to the stove waiting for the tea to boil. He said to Charan Singh, "Now you watch the tea while I go and take a quick shower myself."

They had their tea and listened to the music. Charan Singh felt totally relaxed. At home, under the watchful eyes of his son or daughter-in-law, he was always afraid that he might say or do something to upset them. But here he felt like he was in his own home back in the village.

Jawala Singh prepared dinner like a skilled chef. He speedily kneaded the flour and made rotis and wrapped them neatly in a pona, a small piece of cloth, which he placed in a small rattan basket. Then he put a pot of chicken curry on the stove to heat. He asked Charan Singh to grab the bottle of whisky from the bedroom.

Jawala Singh poured whisky into two large glasses, added some tap water into each glass, and handed one to Charan Singh. Jawala Singh raised the glass a little towards Charan Singh and then quickly downed it. Charan Singh did the same but found it hard to swallow the strong whisky and had to get a drink of water to soothe his throat. They finished the bottle while they ate their roti.

Whether it was the effect of the whisky or the relaxed ambience of Jawala Singh's home, Charan Singh wanted it to last for ever. Their conversation turned to their present situation and Charan Singh started to complain about his family, as he had done many times before. "Jawala Singh, our home was the most happy place one can imagine. My son was the best . . ."

Jawala Singh interrupted him. "Listen, you can go on torturing yourself like this forever if you like, but it is not going to change a thing for you. If it was just your son, we could find fault in him, but don't you see, here in Canada, most people are like that."

"I am not against his business or wealth. I never even ask for anything from him. All I want now is that he should have his mother live with him, keep the family together, be part of the family like in the old days. Why has he become so indifferent? This is what bothers me and this is what I can't understand."

"And you will never understand it. For me, I have simply stopped thinking about these matters. It is so peaceful now. I'm the king in my own castle."

"Yes, you are right."

"I am telling you this again, you are welcome to come and stay here with us. Don't keep on hoping that your son will do something for you.

"My wife was never able to get along with our daughter-in-law. There was always friction in the house so we decided to move out. We had a reasonably happy life on our own for as long as she was alive. When she died my son asked me to move back in with him. But I didn't like it there and rented this basement. My son sometimes comes around and even brings my grandchildren to meet me. I go to his house on special occasions. It's quite straightforward, really—if you get along, then nothing like it, but if not, then why bother each other?"

Charan Singh looked at the falling snow outside his window. He knew that Jawala Singh would not go to work today. He thought of doing the same, but then he realized that it was Saturday and his daughter-in-law would be home all day and she would make him uncomfortable one way or another.

He thought about Jawala Singh's offer and said to himself, Maybe I should go and live with him. Then he became fearful of that thought. How can one leave one's own home? He asked himself another question, Is this really my home?

He got up at five-thirty. His whole body ached. Slowly he opened the door and went into the bathroom. The hot water felt comfortable. He put on his work clothes, which he had kept in the bathroom. They felt frozen. He tied his turban, put on his large jacket, and covered the turban with the hood. He put on his big rubber boots and picked his lunch kit, which lay by the wall where his daughter-in-law had placed it last night. He knew the contents: two egg sandwiches, a banana, and two cookies.

Slowly and noiselessly he opened the rear basement door. It was not easy walking in knee-deep fresh snow. He walked by the side of the house and arrived at the front road. He stopped for a moment and looked at the house. With snow on the rooftop the house looked beautiful. He quickly started to walk towards the bus stop, but after a few steps he put down his lunch kit on the snow to fix his turban under the hood of his jacket.

Everything had turned white under the blanket of snow. He stood still for a while with his lunch kit in his hand, and then, instead of going to the bus stop he started to walk towards Jawala Singh's house, which was a little more than a mile away.

The decision made him feel good and the crackling sound of the snow under his feet sounded like a beautiful song. After a short distance, he stopped and looked back with interest at his own footprints. He resumed walking with long happy steps, enjoying the song of the crisp snow under his feet.

A New Job for Dale

B HAI-JI, HAVE A DRINK FIRST. We'll talk later."

"Look, Dale, don't be an idiot, it's only nine in the morning and you are already drunk."

"Bhai-ji, you are one hundred percent right in that. I agree. But you don't understand, I got a new job."

"Now listen! Go home, take a good shower and sleep. Come to work tomorrow morning. We are loaded with work this week."

"I don't want to work on cars anymore, Bha-ji. Try to understand. I got a new job, first class."

"Look at yourself. You can't even stand still. After just one drink, your body starts to shake all over. Eat some healthy food once in a while."

"I know I don't have a big wrestler's body like you do, but don't worry about me, I am like steel, I never break. Come on, have a drink with me. Don't you consider my happiness as your happiness? Have at least one drink."

"It's hard to get mad at you, you know. You mix your Hindi, Punjabi, and English in a way that makes no sense and you swing like a bamboo tree when you talk. You make me laugh every time."

"Bhai-ji, my elders went to Fiji from Punjab. Most people spoke Hindi there, so they started to speak Hindi. Now in Canada we speak English."

"I know that your elders went from Punjab, and your name is Sardar Daljit Singh Dhillon, but it sounds so funny, the way you mix everything."

"Laugh, sure, go ahead laugh at me, Bhai-ji, after all you are my big brother. But laugh with happiness for me today, not at me."

"I don't know what you are happy about."

"Now you are talking. Have a piece of this fried chicken with the drink. I brought it especially for you. What do you think of the drink? It's home-made stuff, number one, first class."

"Where did you get it?"

"I'll tell you everything in a minute, don't worry. Have a little more."

"You are not gonna let me do any work today, are you?"

"Arrey Bhai-ji, you are the king, what you care? Look at me, I have nothing, I own nothing, still I am on top of the world. Come tell me about the drink, eh?"

"Yea it's good, made by a real pro, I can tell."

"He is a special guy. Not just the drink, I'll be getting a lot more from him, you just wait and see. I must have done some good deeds in my last incarnation. This good life is my karma. Here, have a bit more."

"Not too much, Kanjjra, I haven't eaten anything this morning. It is Friday today, you should have come in the evening, we could have had a good party."

"We will drink in the evening too. We are not going to do keertan in the evening, are we? We're the kings, you and me. We don't need anybody's permission to drink. And today is a special day anyway."

"You just keep on jabbering away and haven't told me a damn thing yet. You talk like you've found some rich lady to marry or something."

"It's something like that. Yes, there is a marriage involved in this."

"First you told me you got a job and now you are talking about marriage as well. Dale, you're losing it, man."

"Yea, it sounds a bit confused even to me. It is a job and it is also a marriage arrangement. I'll tell you everything, have another drink."

"Okay, I'll pour myself this time, now you start telling me about this job of yours. I want to know what kind of lottery you have won here."

"What are lotteries anyway, it is only money. I've got better news than that."

"Start your story, you bastard, or I'm gonna beat the hell out of you."

"Now don't get angry at me, Bhai-ji. I'll tell you all about it. Arrey, look at the time, it's getting late. My boss should be coming back soon as well."

"Who is this boss you are talking about?"

"The same guy who just dropped me here, he is my boss."

"You bastard, you worked for me for so long, never called me boss?"

"You are not my boss, you are my Bhai-ji, my dear big brother. I love you Bhai-ji."

"Isn't he the same person you rented the basement from?"

"The very same person. I still live in his basement."

"But you used to tell me that he was a very fanatical religious type."

"Yea, he used to talk Khalistan and all that, but not any more. He is a real good drinking buddy. He is the one who hired me."

"Hired you for what?"

"Wah-wah, this drink is the real thing, man, it leaves a special kind of taste in your mouth, have another one."

"Slow down, you bastard. You will be falling flat in a few minutes if you keep this up."

"We've been drinking since last night. Now I'm gonna go home and sleep. But I told my boss that I must see my Bhai-ji. I told him I have to discuss something very important with my brother, so I came."

"But you haven't told me anything."

"I was about to tell you. So my boss said, Dale Sahib, you enjoy your life on my account. And I said, Well, let's do that. How can I object to something like that eh?"

"Go on and sit straight in the chair, don't fall off!"

"You don't know your brother Dale, do you? I don't fall that easy."

"And blow your smoke on the other side, goddamn you."

"You really dislike cigarettes, my boss on the other hand . . . "

"Okay, are you going to tell me your story, or do I have to throw you out of my office?"

"All right, Bhai-ji, now I tell you everything. So this boss of mine said to me, 'Dale, I've got a job for you.' I say, 'What is the job, Bhai Sahib?' He said, 'I'll tell you about the job, first you say yes.' I say 'Okay boss,' then he said, 'You know how my wife always fights with me.' 'That is very true,' I said."

"How do you know they always fight with each other?"

"I know everything. He drinks and curses her brothers. She throws him out of the house. He comes and stays with me every time."

"Doesn't she slap you a few times as well?"

"Why would she do that? I pay her big rent and look after her drunk husband most of the time. You don't know her, Bhai-ji, she is one very smart woman. She usually has everything all figured out in advance. Anyway, you don't worry about me, no one dare beat me."

"You are right, a slap would probably kill you, and who wants to go to jail for that?"

"Sure, go laugh at me, Bhai-ji, I don't mind. So anyway, my boss said to me, 'Dale, I want to teach my wife a lesson,' and he told me that when he went to India last year he secretly married another woman there."

"Get out of here. He seems to be a sensible man."

"Yea, he seems to be, but he isn't. I tell you. Bhai-ji, you think that anybody who wears a turban is a pious soul. It's not like that at all. This man seems okay from the outside, but inside he is something else."

"So he told no one that he got married again in India?"

"No one but me."

"You mean he has been living with his wife ever since he came back from India and hasn't told her anything?"

"Exactly. You are such a straight man, Bhai-ji, straight like a phone pole, you have no idea what people are up to nowadays. Both man and wife hide things from each other. This is how it is, Bhai-ji. Let's have another drink now."

"First tell me the whole story."

"The story is complete. Now he wants me to sponsor this other wife so she can come to Canada. In other words I am going to apply to Immigration."

"So this is your new job?"

"Yes! Now what do you say, isn't this a matter for celebration? I will have the time of my life until she comes. He makes the best moonshine there is. He will give me money to spend. What else do I need?"

"And if you get into trouble?"

"What trouble, Bhai-ji? People go scot-free after committing murder here. All I'm gonna do is just lie a little to the immigration department. In a way it is not really a lie either. I am not married."

"I have told you to get married many times, but you don't listen."

"No, I don't want to get married again, once was enough. That is it. But really, Bhai-ji, that stupid woman, my wife, did me a lot of harm."

"She did nothing to you. The way you tried to beat her up every time you got drunk, she should have killed you."

"So what? Don't other people do that? My father and his father before him did that. I hear in Punjab everyone used to beat their wives. No, Bhai-ji, it is just that the whole goddamn chakkar, the system, in Canada is different. Women have no respect for their husbands anymore."

"Dale, you should be thankful that your wife was a decent person. She listened to us and forgave you, otherwise you would probably still be in jail today."

"Arrey, Bhai-ji why do you want to spoil this time of my happiness by talking about old things, eh? Have a last drink, my boss will come in a minute, and I'll be out of here."

"Never mind the drink. Think about this seriously. If his wife's brother came around and broke your legs, what will you do then? If you have any sense, stay away from this man."

"I am in it already, Bhai-ji, he has given me five thousand dollars cash and he will give another five thousand when that woman comes to Canada."

"But this is not right, Dale. You shouldn't be getting into

these kinds of things!"

"You're such a noble soul, you won't understand. That is why I respect you so much. Even when you call me names, I say nothing. Actually you are the one who should wear a turban."

"Shut up and listen. What you're doing is illegal and it's morally wrong to deceive people."

"Bhai-ji, who knows who is deceiving whom? What do we know about that woman from India? She might have her own plans? Otherwise who would marry a man like my boss, without knowing anything about him? Now tell me that?"

"I am only concerned about you."

"I know, Bhai-ji. You never say anything wrong. But what do I have to lose? I will have a good life for a while, free drinks and all. We will see what happens after that. Oh, here comes my boss now. So should I bring more drinks in the evening?"

"No, but come back when you are sober and we will talk more about this."

"Don't worry about me, Bhai-ji, na kisi ke ham, na koi mera, I care for no one, no one cares for me. I will have fun for a few days, what else is left in this world for me?"

"You come back tomorrow, you understand, we will talk."

"You are such a nice person, Bhai-ji, but don't worry about me. Tell me, do you know anybody else who ever got such a wonderful job? It is a matter of kismet, Bhai-ji. See, my boss is waiting for me. So long, Bhai-ji, my big brother."

"Walk slowly, be careful, you're gonna hurt yourself . . . "

The Accident

BHAI-JI, THE SIKH PRIEST of the local gurdwara, quickly finished his tea. It was already eight forty-five in the morning and he wanted to stop at the gurdwara before going to the funeral home. He hastily readjusted his turban and checked the long line of buttons on his Nehru jacket, wrapped his saffron-coloured piece of ceremonial cloth around his neck, and combed his long, flowing, grey beard with his fingers. After tying his shoelaces, he stopped for a brief moment but suppressed the idea of purifying his hands and swiftly went out of the house.

It was not snowing this morning, but the presence of the white stuff all around was enough to make Bhai-ji shiver with cold. Bhai-ji dashed to the car which his daughter had already started, and as soon as he stepped in he said to her, "Beta, hurry up, we have to go to the gurdwara for a few minutes before going to the funeral home."

Sleepy and tired and feeling annoyed, she said, "Bapu-ji, you won't be able to get to the funeral home on time, don't blame me after."

Bhai-ji looked again confidently at his watch. He desperately wanted to see Beant Singh, who was having the akhandpath, a religious ceremony, at the gurdwara this morning. His daughter had worked the graveyard shift so he did not insist, but he blamed his own situation for not being able to afford another car.

The roads had been cleared and salted overnight. Bhai-ji, lost in thought, was looking outside but he did not see the soft fresh snow on the rooftops and tree branches. This morning his assignment was to go to the local funeral home and perform two last rites for the dead, one at nine-thirty and the other at eleven-thirty. The first rite was for Sardar Khushhal Singh's mother, which he didn't want to miss. This was a God-given opportunity to show his loyalty to Khushhal Singh, who had helped him settle in Canada and got him the job in the gurdwara.

The problem was the second rite. Bhai-ji wanted to be at the gurdwara before twelve, when the final ceremony of akhandpath is performed. However, he could not refuse performing the rite; the religious rituals that follow the rite could then easily pass to the other gurdwara, and the committee would never tolerate such a loss. Bhai-ji had to be very careful. These days the majority of the committee was made up of very hot-tempered Sikhs who were always at-the-ready to "unsheathe the sword" at the slightest disagreement. The ongoing political problems in Punjab that had caused Bhai-ji to flee to Canada continued to affect his life here.

Just to keep his job at the gurdwara, he had to do duties not normally demanded of a granthi, the Sikh priest. He had to change the colour of his turban from blue to orange, the colour preferred by militant sikhs. He had pictures of gurus and saints in his home, but now he must hang the picture of the saint Bhinderan Wala, who was killed by the Indian army in Amritsar. A close relative of a very powerful committee member had come from India and was anxious to get Bhai-ji's position.

To make things worse, the head granthi did not like him very much and had the power to fire him anytime. That is how the poor fellow, whom Bhai-ji replaced, had lost his job. He was an educated young man who rejected old practices based on Hindu mythology. It was customary for people to donate clothes, quilts, and pillows in the names of their dead relatives so they could be comfortable in their next life. The head granthi sold these items back to the stores where they were bought. The junior granthi protested, "It is useless to give comforters and pillows for the dead. This is not what our gurus told us." The head granthi saw this as an attack on his authority and fired the junior.

Bhai-ji had seriously thought about quitting this work altogether. But what else could he do? He had never done any kind of physical work in his life. He was not going to work as a janitor or farm worker at his age now. He lamented not starting a business, especially when he thought about the great success his friend Jaswant Singh had had in his business.

Jaswant Singh had been earning very little, doing freelance path-reading shifts at local gurdwaras or in people's homes. He was envious of Bhai-ji's permanent position. Out of desperation, Jaswant Singh started his own business. He offered full-package akhandpaths in people's homes—the Guru Granth Sahib, a compact sound system, handkerchiefs to cover the attendees' heads, incense, cooking utensils, and so on. His family members did the path-reading shifts and the keertan at the conclusion of the akhandpath. His younger son even sang the religious songs accompanied by the toomba, the single-string instrument. He charged a lump sum for this entire service package. People were happy because it saved them the time and headache of arranging everything separately. Jaswant Singh made a lot of money and paid no taxes. In a short time, he bought a big home for his family and a rental property.

Bhai-ji was earning a good wage, no doubt, and he received private donations from well-wishers, but it was nothing compared to Jaswant Singh's financial success. Bhai-ji laid most of the blame on his own family. His elder son had fallen in bad company and started to drink publicly. In order to save his job, Bhai-ji had to throw him out of the house.

Bhai-ji didn't always see his life as a failure. He remembered the immense happiness he felt when he was able to get a permanent immigrant status in Canada. He had come with a religious hymn-singing group, and had remained here illegally. With the help of some influential people in the community, he was able to stay. It was the greatest achievement of his life. Soon he brought his family to Canada. Being a granthi in the gurdwara was not just a job to him, it was a service to the community. In those days he often said, "Waheguru, God, has given me this opportunity to serve the sangat, the congregation, for which I am eternally grateful to Him." Bhai-ji believed what he preached about money, greed, and their terrible effects on humans.

Things changed. Bhai-ji felt left behind. He still lived in a small old home, while many newcomers had bigger homes and better cars. Often he experienced a great desire to be at the same level as the others. Today was one of those days. Since the early morning, his mind had been in constant upheaval.

The car stopped in front of the funeral home and Bhai-ji silently stepped out. George Harding, the funeral home attendant, greeted him. Bhai-ji knew him well and was comfortable with him, compared to the other white workers there. George walked in front of him and through the narrow hall; they entered a small, spotlessly clean room. As always, Bhai-ji found the room warm but uncomfortable.

Khushhal Singh came into the room soon after. For a few moments, they both stood in complete silence, then Bhai-ji put his hand on Khushhal Singh's shoulder and said, "Have faith in the doings of the Lord, Sardar-ji. Make your heart strong. Remember, everything happens according to God's command."

"You are our only hope Bhai-ji," said Khushhal Singh.

"Sardar Khushhal Singh-ji, we can only hope from the One Above." Bhai-ji sat down on a chair near the small table and they talked for a while.

After Khushhal Singh left the room, George brought in another man. He was the son of Nirmal Singh, the deceased man whose funeral was at eleven-thirty. He gave Bhai-ji the necessary information about his father and left as quietly as he had come in.

Sitting in the room Bhai-ji could hear the footsteps of people walking into the chapel where the service was to be held. He knew that Khushhal Singh's relatives, business associates, clients, and other acquaintances would come in large numbers and the small chapel would be filled in no time. A number of people would have to stand outside in the snow. Bhai-ji thought about their discomfort and blamed the funeral home owners. He didn't like many other things about this place, especially the enormous fees they charged. Converting dollars into rupees, Bhai-ji would get very angry. He considered it daylight robbery by the white people.

His thoughts were interrupted when George came to inform him that it was time to start the service. Bhai-ji slowly walked to the microphone. To his right, the body of Naranjan Kaur lay in the best coffin that the funeral home had available. Her head was wrapped in a white chunni, a scarf. A flower bouquet was placed close to her hands on the unopened part of the box.

He began by quoting from the Holy Granth: "Ghale aaei Nanka, sadey uthey jai." Birth and death are the will of God. On other occasions, he would spend considerable time on these matters, but today he moved rapidly to shed light on the glorious life of Sardar Khushhal Singh's mother: "Mata Naranjan Kaur was a truly great soul. She gave us a gem of a person, Sardar Khushhal Singh, who has taken our community to new heights. As many of you know, he came as a visitor to this country, but with hard work and a most remarkable personality, Sardar Sahib has become the owner of many homes, apartments, and other properties, enhancing our community in the eyes of white people. He has always helped a person in need. I am pleased to tell you that Sardar-ji helped me get immigrant status and later found jobs for members of my family. We are all proud of the fact that Sardar Khushhal Singh is a jewel in our community."

Bhai-ji was pleased to see the satisfied look on the face of Sardar Khushhal Singh, sitting in the front row. Then he eyed the entire congregation from one end to the other to measure the effect of his lecture on them. For a brief moment they seemed like lifeless figurines placed on rows of benches. He shouted the Sikh religious slogan, "Jo bole so nihal"—all those who speak will be blessed. The sangat responded, "Sat sri akaal."

The next speaker was a tall, slim, turbaned man. Walking towards the mike, he adjusted his tie and brushed his mustache back. Like Bhai-ji, he started with a quote from the Gurbani and went into great details about his close relationship with Khushhal Singh and his family.

Bhai-ji repeatedly looked at his watch. He thought that the man's speech was long and boring compared to his own. Another stream of thought began in his mind, as he compared himself with another granthi, Labh Singh. He felt superior to Labh Singh on moral grounds. Labh Singh enjoyed drinking and socializing, and there were times when even Bhai-ji secretly had had a few drinks with him. Eventually, for his impious behaviour, the committee fired Labh Singh.

After being kicked out of his position from the gurdwara, Labh Singh went through rough times. Bhai-ji felt genuine sympathy for him. Then a completely unexpected thing happened. As they say: a kick intended to hurt a hunchback, helped him. Labh Singh started to perform keertan and katha, hymn-singing and preaching, in people's homes. The sermons he preached were meant to impress upon his listeners how important it was to have these sessions in their homes. With the help of some like-minded people, Labh Singh became an instant celebrity. Bhai-ji was astonished to hear that women were lining up to massage and rub Labh Singh's legs, as if he were a famous saint with mystical powers. Sometimes Bhai-ji imagined himself sitting in Labh Singh's place with beautiful women rubbing his legs and thighs, and the tension from his body evaporating. But after such a thought, Bhai-ji felt deep guilt and denounced the actions of Labh Singh as corrupt and immoral.

When Bhai-ji's thoughts returned to the present, the speaker was finishing his remarks: "I want to close by saying that not every mother is fortunate enough to give birth to people like our dear Sardar Khushhal Singh."

It was time for the prayer. Bhai-ji took off his shoes and held in his hands the piece of saffron cloth that hung from his neck, and started the prayer. While reciting the prayer he worried in his mind that it was taking a long time for the people to walk past the coffin for a final glimpse of Mata Naranjan Kaur. He knew that except for a few close relatives, most of the people were not there for a last glimpse, rather they were there to show their faces to Sardar Khushhal Singh. Bhai-ji felt a bad taste in his mouth over this collective hypocrisy.

Bhai-ji looked at his watch, impatiently but discreetly, while the body was taken to the crematorium across the street where two more prayers were held, before and after the body was finally pushed into the furnace.

To return to the chapel from the crematorium for the second funeral, George gave Bhai-ji a set of car keys and pointed to a car, "Mr Khushal gave these for you. He told me that you needed a car to go back to the gurdwara." Bhai-ji took the keys and felt very important, because Sardar Khushhal Singh had remembered his request.

"Mr Khushal must be a big man in your community, look how many people came to his mother's funeral," said George. Any other time Bhai-ji could have talked endlessly in praise of Sardar Khushhal Singh, but now he simply nodded his agreement. George readily agreed to Bhai-ji's suggestion to speed up the process for the next service. He too wanted to finish the whole thing as quickly as possible to avoid paying overtime to his employees.

The body of Nirmal Singh was placed in a very simple-looking wooden box. In addition to his close relatives there were a few elderly men who had worked with him in the Fraser Valley farms. Bhai-ji knew many of these people and detested them with a passion. He was tired of seeing their faces at every funeral. He looked at his watch, anxious to get the service over with in order to get to the gurdwara in time.

Bhai-ji quickly finished the prayer. Nirmal Singh's wife let out a heart-searing wail and Bhai-ji and many others in the chapel realized for the first time that they had come to witness the last rites of the departed. Nirmal Singh's son helped his mother come closer to the box. She lightly pressed the cold fingers of her dead husband and tried to move away, gathering all her courage. After a couple of steps she turned back and again held her husband's hands and cried, "Who's going to look after me, now that you are gone . . . " Overcome with emotion, her body went limp. While her relatives helped her back to her seat, Bhai-ji looked again at his watch and wished that they would hurry up.

Back at the crematorium, going through all the prayers, Bhai-ji found it hard to stay focused. He was annoyed with his daughter. If only she had taken me to the gurdwara for a few minutes this morning. I just wanted to inform Sardar Beant Singh that I would be a little late.

With every passing minute Bhai-ji felt that he was losing his golden opportunity to show loyalty to Beant Singh by praising him in front of the sangat. Beant Singh owned a big farm in the Fraser Valley and had given Bhai-ji's wife a full season's worth of UIC stamps, even though she had not worked a single day. He had promised to give a permanent job of driving a tractor to Bhai-ji's nephew, who was still illegal in the country. Bhai-ji was also hoping to use Beant Singh's help to sponsor a young relative from India, and for numerous other things.

It was already close to twelve when Bhai-ji was finally able to get out of the crematorium. He was the first one to emerge from the building, and once outside he ran to the car holding his ceremonial cloth in his right hand. He slammed on the pedal as soon as he turned into Fraser Street but had to stop at the traffic light on Forty-first Avenue. He cursed loudly, as he was all alone in the car now. Though it was Sunday, there were a lot of cars on the street, or at least that is what it seemed. A couple of times he did not even stop for the pedestrians where he should have.

The reading on the speedometer was over eighty kilometers per hour when the car hit a pole at Fifty-seventh Avenue while trying to make a left turn.

Beant Singh's akhandpath had just been concluded when the news came that Bhai-ji had died in a car accident just a few blocks away from the gurdwara.

Farmer Jerry

A S JERRY TURNED HIS PICKUP on to the road from his strawberry fields, the sharp evening sun blinded him. He pulled the visor down and checked the time—it was already after seven. Suddenly he felt tired. He had been up since five and it had been a long hot day.

He took his baseball cap off and threw it onto the cluttered passenger seat. He moved the rear-view mirror and looked at his tired face below the forehead—it was dark and dirty. He returned the rear-view mirror to its original position and put the cap back on his head.

He was especially edgy today. He had to go to the city to get a tractor spare part, but there were still pickers in the fields. Previously he had been a contractor and knew quite well that a contractor's main concern was the number of flats picked not how well the job was done. Contractors brought in more than half the pickers in his fields. It was not easy to get money from the canneries when there were leaves and other junk mixed in with the strawberries.

Whenever there was a problem with the machinery or some unplanned chore to be done in the city, mostly he was forced to go himself. Last week he sent a new worker on a small errand. The fellow spent an hour looking for the place and wasted the whole day on a task that Jerry himself could have done in forty minutes. On top of that he had put a big dent on the side of the pickup. He told the man not to show his face on the farm again and felt better when he made a joke about his university degrees from Punjab.

Jerry fondly called his pickup *The Wind* and loved it more than anything else in his life. His great-grandfather had named his horse *The Wind*. Jerry often spent hours washing and waxing the truck, but during the berry-picking season he hardly had time to wash his own face.

He turned into the private road leading to his palacelike house, built on a small hill that was visible for miles around. Watching his house from a distance, he often recalled the dark basement where he had lived with his friends when new in this country. He used to dream of a big home. The house he built was way bigger than in his dreams. Around it were a park with tennis courts and a huge pool, which he always described as "my pool."

Seeing his son playing tennis with his girlfriend, Jerry swore in anger. "This is the busiest season and the bastard is playing tennis with his white girlfriend, as if he belongs to the Royal family." His daughter Sandy also, ever since she entered university, didn't come close to the farm let alone help at home.

He parked his truck in the garage. The big doors to the three-car garage were always left open during the summer. Quickly he got out and threw his cap on a shelf. He sat on the steps leading up into the house to take his shoes off. His wife, Binder, who had come home just minutes before him, was already in the kitchen preparing the evening meal. She got up an hour before him every morning, cooked breakfast, and packed their lunch bags. Hearing him, she promptly came from the kitchen and stood in the doorway. She said, "The union people were here. They brought this paper and they are going to talk to the workers in the cabins again."

Jerry angrily grabbed the paper. "How many times have I told you not to open the door when they come! Will you ever learn?"

"Don't shout at me! I just came in from the fields a few minutes ago. They handed it to Nick."

He saw the annoyance in his wife's eyes and decided to be quiet. In the past Jerry would have slapped her a few times for speaking back. Following their marriage, for years he used to beat her up whenever he felt like, just as his father and grandfather had done to their wives. Things had changed now. He blamed his daughter for this. An incident happened three years ago when Sandy was in her last year of high school, a very active and mature seventeen-year-old. He came home drunk after spending the afternoon at a friend's farm. As usual he expected that Binder would place the dinner in front of him immediately. She shocked him by telling him to take his own food from the kitchen and went off to the bedroom. Angrily he went after her and slapped her a couple of times. Sandy happened to be in her room and came out to see the commotion.

Sandy took her mother to a friend's house and Jerry had to beg them to come home the next day. He signed a written promise that he would not hit Binder again. What surprised and hurt Jerry was that even his son Nick took their side in this matter.

He was back on the road driving to where he had just come from. His wrath now switched from Binder to the union people.

He looked at the notice from the union. At the top of a typed page was the date, Tuesday, June 7, 1982, and the names Sarwan Sahota and Jaswant Grewal were written in blue ink. They were the two organizers who had been coming to his cabins for a number of weeks now.

Workers living in his cabins were mostly elderly, uneducated people from the same region as his own village in Punjab. They all had family connections with each other. A few were related to Jerry's family as well. Most of these new immigrants lived with their sons or daughters in small towns in the interior of British Columbia. A few were from Alberta. Each year they arrived some weeks before the work began in order to secure a place for the season.

Like most farmers in the area, Jerry opposed the union. Through their lawyers, the farmers had made every legal effort to stop the union, and Jerry took an active role in these efforts. He was not worried about the workers in his own cabins. Due to his ties with them, he believed that they would not go against him.

He remembered the confrontation he had had with the organizers when they came to his farm the first time. He was drinking with a contractor in a nearby strawberry field, when his relatives informed him about the union men. Jerry rushed to the cabins and saw a few workers outside their cabins talking to the organizers. They all quickly went inside as soon as they saw him. Jerry hurled abuses at the organizers and they soon gave up and left. He thought they would never show up again.

Later that evening, after a few drinks, he phoned his farmer friend Bikar. He said, "Look, Bikar, you can't be nice with these people. The only thing they understand and respect is power. You have to show them who is the boss." Bikar, a more reasonable person, tried to tell him that it was their legal right to talk to the workers. "No way, as long as I am living I will not let them just walk into my cabins and instigate my pickers against me," was Jerry's reply.

But the union reps were back the following week. He was surprised but tried to engage them in friendly idle talk. They responded in a formal manner, "The courts have given us the permission to speak with farmworkers. And it is you who are breaking the law while we are here. You are not supposed to be here while we talk to the workers."

This made Jerry mad. "You think I give a damn about the law that tells me to stay away from my own home? You can take that piece of paper and stick it you know where. Salleyo, my family has ruled over people like you for generations. No one dared to face my great-grandfather in all the villages."

Sarwan, one of the union reps replied calmly, "You better understand that this is not your village. Stop dreaming you are like your great-grandfather. According to the laws in Canada, workers too have rights. You may be the owner of these cabins, but you don't own the workers."

"Don't live in a fools' paradise, believing the laws. Those who have the power, do the same things here. In my cabins only my rules will be followed. Most of these people are like my family. See for yourself, the minute they saw me, they went into their cabins."

In response Sarwan started speaking loudly as though he were addressing a large rally. He said, "We only want to tell our brothers and sisters that they do the hard work and should be paid a fare wage for their labours."

The second organizer, Jaswant, followed suit. "You sir, charge rent from the workers for these cabins, then why should they follow your rules? They should ask you to clean this place up and make it liveable for humans. Look at these puddles and the mosquitoes around here."

"You are exploiting them in every which way possible, yet you call them your extended family," added Sarwan.

At first Jerry responded similarly but then he realized what they were trying to do. Workers in the cabins could hear everything being said. He changed his tactics and in a very sociable manner he touched Sarwan on the shoulder as a Punjabi friend would. Speaking in a friendly voice, he said, "Listen yaar, we have no reason to fight. We are from the same place, have the same religion, speak the same language. We should join together to fight the white folks for discriminating against us. I try to provide jobs for our people, otherwise where are they going to find work without English. Let's go home. We will have a few drinks and have something to eat. What do you want from these poor folks anyway? You know our people. They are not going to appreciate anything you do."

"Go sell this bullshit to someone else. You are the last person we will have drinks with," was Sarwan's sharp reply.

"We are leaving for now but don't think we won't be back. It is our legal right to be here," Jaswant warned.

"If you dare come this way again, I promise, you will not walk out of here alive!"

They ignored him and went to their car and drove off.

He was surprised at their persistence and each time they came he used every method he could think of to stop them. Each confrontation added to his frustrations.

His thoughts drifted back to his younger days in the village. It seemed to him that he had been in dispute with these types of people all his life. He had not forgotten the time he had to stay away from his village for six months because of "idiot comrades." Jerry's father, grandfather, and most of the other Jat men of the village couldn't understand why there was such a big fuss over a girl from a low caste. In their minds, Jerry hadn't done anything out of the ordinary. Jats, who owned the land in the village, had been using lower-caste women for their sexual pleasure for as long as anybody could remember. All Jerry did was to grab this ugly little thing to have some fun with, as any young Jat man of his age would do.

The girl's father complained to the sarpanch, the head of the village panchayat. The sarpanch, who happened to be Jerry's uncle, tried to settle the matter by offering some money to the family. To his surprise his offer was refused. Eventually, the progressive young men of the village took up the matter. Jerry had to flee to neighbouring UP and stay in hiding for six months. Though he had had a great time at his aunt's farm in UP, he still carried the bitterness he had felt at the time against the "comrades."

These union organizers were the exact copies of those young men from the village. Jerry did everything to oppose them. He used his influence in the local gurdwaras to stop them from speaking there. He even looked for men who could hunt the organizers for a price. He knew a couple of white people who could and would do such a deed for him, but their price was too high.

One day while drinking, one of Jerry's farmer friends, Balwant, said that he had paid a white man five thousand dollars just for breaking the windshield of a union organizer's car. Crying over his spent money, Balwant said, "The amount of money these thugs want for such a job is just too much. And we have to pay the lawyers huge fees. Then you have to keep the contractors happy by offering them drinks everyday. We could actually work out a deal with our workers for half the amount."

"It is not a matter of money alone, Balwant; it is a matter of pride. I am the owner of the farm. I can't let anyone else give me orders as to what I can or cannot do on my own farm. To let them organize my farm would be the biggest insult."

"Jerry, it has nothing to do with insult. In this business the only thing you need to concentrate on is what is in your financial interest. That's all."

"This is the one thing I really hate about this country. There is no real respect here for money or power, the kind we have back home. You can do whatever legal or illegal thing you want, all you have to do is to bribe a few people," said Jerry in a depressing tone. "Back home, we had a couple of young lads from lower-caste families who had worked in our fields for more than two generations. These kids would lay their lives on the line for us at a moment's notice. I haven't been able to find anyone like those two in this place."

"I hear what you are saying, brother. Here you have to do even the dirty work yourself," said Balwant, liquor slurring his speech.

"I have not forgotten what I learned from my grandfather. When I was young, in grade four or five, I had a fight in school. The kid I fought with was a little stronger and he beat me up. My grandfather sat me down and said, "Jarnail, son, you are born in a sardar family, so you have to know how to be one. If you need to fight with someone, never ever do it yourself. Always have someone else do the fighting for you. That is what it means to be a sardar."

Lost in his thoughts, Jerry was unable to figure out what he could do to stop the union. He felt helpless. He wanted to forget his lawyer's advice. He had pleaded with the lawyer, "Mr Simpson, for me, this is a matter of my pride. I just cannot stomach the idea that someone can just walk into my farm without my permission."

The lawyer warned him, "Mr Brar, the first thing you must understand is that your farm is not your home. You don't live there any more; it is your business place. The farmworkers who live in your cabins are not your property like the land or the buildings. They pay rent to you for living there. You cannot legally stop the union organizers from talking to them."

Jerry slowed down his truck. He was already at the approach road to his farm. He recognized the union organizers' car parked near the house in the driveway. He stopped the truck on the main road and looked towards the house but didn't see anyone. "They must be on the other of the cabins, he thought."

He turned the motor off and stretched his tired arms and legs. He raised his feet on the passenger side to be more comfortable. Something hit his right foot and he suddenly remembered that there was half a bottle of scotch left from last week. He picked up the bottle and looked at it for a brief moment. Then he grabbed a small paper cup, quickly filled it with scotch and drank it.

He hadn't eaten anything since lunch, and the liquor had an immediate effect on him. He straightened himself in the seat again and looked towards the cabins. His eyes settled on the old house and he was surprised that he hadn't recently paid any attention to the building. It seemed old and dilapidated. Many years ago when he bought the house with forty acres of land, it had looked attractive. He became "farmer" to all his workers and relatives. Before that everyone knew him as "Contractor Jerry."

The house triggered many old memories. Before moving here from Vancouver, they had lived in his father-in-law's basement for many years. The sawmill he worked for was shut down permanently and he was out of a job. His father-in-law advised him to become a farm contractor. Jerry didn't like the suggestion at first. But with a young family he had no choice. His father-in-law found him an old truck that had been used by a Chinese farmer to transport vegetables to the market. They fixed benches in the truck for the workers to sit on, and he was ready.

But soon after Jerry began taking workers to the Abbotsford farms he changed his mind about this profession. By the end of the first farming season, Jerry knew that he had found the kind of work that he had been dreaming of. He made more money than he ever could working in the sawmill. What pleased him most was the status of his new job. The workers he transported to and from the farms were mostly uneducated older Punjabi immigrants and a few illegal young Punjabis trying to make some money while hoping to get immigrant status in Canada.

In his position he could scold his workers anyway he desired. No one dared to speak in front of him. He had finally found a job that made him equal to his ancestors in possessing power among his own people. With his street smarts he was able to figure out numerous ways to cheat the workers out of their wages or delay payments till the end of the season.

Jerry bought two more vans during the second season. His wife Binder drove one and they hired a young Punjabi immigrant to drive the second one. By the end of the third season he was able to buy forty acres of land and this house that stood by the road.

He continued to work as a contractor, but the new title "Farmer Jerry" delighted him beyond anything. He often said to his wife and kids, "Compared to the contractor, the real boss is the farmer. Everyone is afraid of the big boss."

Many workers who lived in his cabins during the season came from small towns like Williams Lake, Quesnel, and

Prince George, and some came even from Calgary. In the off-season he would travel to these places to personally deliver the money owed to his workers. After such a trip he would tell his wife Binder, "When I go to these people's homes, everybody runs around me like I am the Raja of Patiala." Then he would get sentimental: "I wish my grandfather were alive. He would have loved to see me rule the lives of so many people just as he did in his time."

And now he felt his empire was in danger. He sincerely believed that it was his hereditary right to rule the lives of the people who worked for him and the union was trying to take away that right.

In anger he looked towards his house again and took another large drink from the bottle. He took his cap off and ran his hand through his hair. His hand touched the hunting rifle on the rack behind his head. He turned around and saw the rifle as if for the first time. He took it off the rack and blew the dust from it. This was his favourite rifle. At the end of each season he often went deer hunting with his friends.

He stopped cleaning the rifle, and realized with shock that he was sitting in his truck while the union organizers were in the cabins talking to his workers. He put aside the rifle on the passenger seat, started the pickup and drove towards the cabins.

He saw that the union organizers were talking to the workers in two different groups. Jerry left the pickup running and got out with the rifle in his right hand. The workers started going to their cabins when they heard the vehicle approach. In a few seconds most of them were inside their cabins. A teenage boy, however, remained with the organizers. An elderly man stood by a cherry tree leaning on his walking stick, watching everything with interest.

Jerry's eyes burned with anger and the effect of the scotch.

He looked at the boy and immediately recognized him. The boy had come to live with his sister in the cabin just a few days ago. Jerry had eyes on the sister and he had been trying to befriend the boy ever since he arrived. But now he didn't care, he threatened the boy, "What the hell are you doing, still standing around? Go to your cabin if you know what is good for you, little boy. If you are not gone in a few seconds I"ll beat the shit out of you with my rifle."

But the boy took a step forward and said, "Be careful what you say, don't think that I am just a little kid."

"Go fuck yourself and stay with your brothers-in-law then," Jerry insulted, pointing his rifle in the direction of the union organizers. "If you don't leave my place right now, I am going to kill you both."

But they stood their ground and watched Jerry in amazement. There was not a sound to be heard, even the birds on the trees were quiet.

Before anybody could say or do anything, the young man quickly went to stand with the union organizers. He took the union poster and held it high in his hand.

The old man now energetically walked towards them, saying in an excited voice, "Well done, young man! I am with you too. Let this bastard shoot us all."

Jerry stood there dumbfounded. He lowered his gun and slowly walked away. He stopped and turned for a moment to say, "I will fix each one of you. I wasn't born yesterday. I know how to take care of people like you."

He went and sat in his pickup. Slowly, he turned his truck around and drove away. Through his rear-view mirror he saw that one by one the workers were coming out of their cabins.

Glossary

Ambarsar: Amritsar
akhandpath: a rite consisting of the reading of the Granth
bapu: father
bhai: brother
bhaiaa/ bhaya: Father
chakkar: rotation
chamaar or *chuhrra:* untouchable castes
chunny: scarf
dalaan: big room
dhiey: used to address a daughter
gurdwara: Sikh temple
Granth: the Sikh Holy Book
granthi: Sikh priest
gur: jaggery
Gurbani: Sikh sacred verses
guru-ghar: Guru's home
Jat: land-owning caste
ji: suffix of respect
kanjjra: casual curse
kara: bracelet worn by Sikh men
karah: pudding prepared with granulated wheat, sugar and butter
katha: story, also religious story
keertan: hymn singing

khel: game
ki haal ai: how are you
kurta: shirt
massy: mother's sister
panchayat: village council
rajai: quilt
roti: chapati
Saab: honorific
sala: brother-in-law; also a term of abuse
salleyo: curse
sangat: the congregation
sarpanch: the village head
sat sri akaal: Sikh greeting
toomba: the single-string instrument
veh: casual way of addressing males by women
vidaygee: seeing off
Waheguru: God
wah wah: bravo
yaar: friend